T0197008

TWENTY CENTS

ALEX SPENCER

TWENTY CENTS

iUniverse books may be ordered through booksellers or by contacting:

iUniverse
1663 Liberty Drive
Bloomington, IN 47403
www.iuniverse.com
1-800-Authors (1-800-288-4677)

ISBN: 978-1-5320-4717-6 (sc)
ISBN: 978-1-5320-4754-1 (e)

Library of Congress Control Number: 2018904465

Print information available on the last page.

iUniverse rev. date: 04/09/2018

CHAPTER
ONE

It was a cold rainy morning and it was like any other. I wanted to drive home from my job at Wal-Mart after a two hour shift. I always thought of myself as a hard worker growing up on a farm and making money. I didn't need stuff that I thought I needed. I did a lot of sports so I was always fit. I also went for a lot of walks. I love shopping and going for walks with my German Sheppard. I am a soft gentle soul with my ocean blue eyes, Irish heritage and long flowing hair like my brother. My mom on the other hand has gray hair and dyes it red. I'm a guy that loves the smell of coffee in the morning, maybe a little too much. The thick aroma of Arabica beans and rich deep grounds that make you want another cup of energy is the way that I grew up. Energy drives this country on the backbone of what we are and what we have accomplished as a nation. It was sad that I never had time for my wife and the wife in turn gambled. I never took care of the son and I never wanted to turn them away. I also didn't want my son to have a mental illness either. I always watched sports center and it was the tradeoff. I was addicted to working out and it was something that was a ritual. My wife was addicted to shopping and she loved buying shoes and gift cards. She would take out thousands of dollars on credit cards to spend and I wouldn't have time to pay them off. After a while I would say you made the mess now mop it up. It was raining cats and dogs and the kids at were home with my babysitter with the wife running late for an appointment. We live in a small town where crime thrives and cops make money. We live for money and make greed our second nature. Ravensdale was something you could never get away from and we named it Ravensdale because we considered the raven our bird of peace. We saw ravens as peace and harmony in our town. We welcomed them with open arms and grace among the people. I had a feeling the serial killer knew the law in and out with a criminal books in his nice house. I was going to pay her an extra twenty dollars because she was going to have to reschedule her doctor's appointment. It wasn't a big deal to her but it was to me. I worked the day shift and my wife was running late. She was a half hour behind running errands. She was buying groceries and going to the bank. I thought she should have planned accordingly since I was at work and I couldn't get off work. It was a hassle for her and me too so why did she have to make up so many excuses? It was her job after work it seemed but it was something for her to do. I was a cop but I after ten years I retired because I was tired of the streets. I was tired of getting shot at with all the junkies and the drug busts. I read in the paper about all the arsons and all the dead hookers. If you looked at our town you would realize how bad it really was. Putting away the bad guys and dealing with the shootings and the junkies with the needles in their arms is just routine in our town. I was the cop that played bad cop in the interviews because I was good at it. Most of them didn't ask for a lawyer because most of them wanted to confess to the bad cop or mister sincere cop that wanted to help you. I was the bad cop that got people to confess as a scare tactic. They said I was the best in my division and we had a lot of cop chases and a lot of drug busts. It was in California pulling people over and finding drugs, frisking people and finding drugs. Then I got that call that no father wanted to get, my son was out drinking. It was far away from home and he was hanging with his friends and decided to get a hotel for a night. He got shot by someone when he was on the third floor and the perpetrator was wearing a mask. He was killed with the rest of his friends and my son fell from the third floor and died from the fall. This hotel was five star. We could still smell the blood in the air and believe me it didn't smell like roses. There were always gunshots and sirens all around us but that was normal for our town. It was investigated by the cops and the perpetrator left coins on the eyes on all the victims. I thought it was funny that my son drank because he never drank even with friends. They found no fingerprints on the coins and they think the serial killer had killed them a couple hours after they had entered the room. I don't see why the serial killer waited so long and didn't kill them right then and there. It was sad really, to know that the boys were just looking to have a good time and they were killed by a random act of violence. I remember playing catch with my son, throwing the old pig skin around. There was something that said I needed to get him back and not let him die in vain. This serial killer was part of me now whether I liked it or not. I was always going to think of him of the killer of my son. I wanted him to die and I wanted my son to be alive still having a good time with his friends. I wondered to myself how many people he had killed before he came to make this town. I soon feared he was going to kill the whole town. Was he going to make the headlines for killing drug dealers and firefighters or was he going to kill an artist that was famous like Van Gogh? I don't think it was a random act, I think they knew I was a cop and I knew I wanted his head on a platter. Hopefully the cops caught up with him and made him pay for all his crimes. I wanted the killer behind bars and I wanted him to think about the crime for the rest of his miserable life. In my time as a cop I thought that he had killed before and I think that he was going to kill until he got caught. They were swamped with murder cases and when I told them to talk to talk to my brother in Florida to see if he had killed in Florida. It was confirmed that he had killed in Florida. After that connection was made we were happy with it and we said this was finally something we could run with. Florida was a cozy warm place where you could drink a cold overpriced beer and an icy margarita. There were a lot of killings in the paper. They were mostly hookers and cops and school kids. It was a tragedy that so many people had to die especially school kids and cops. Hookers were people too but they weren't mentioned much like the kids and cops. There were good reading in those pages but they didn't put the big details in the paper because they didn't want the serial killer to get wind of what we were getting from these cases. They didn't put the gun make or the bullets used or anything like that. They also didn't have any suspects. There were tips coming in non stop but most of them weren't panning out. Some seemed to lead to places that were helpful and going to places you never thought to look. It's one of those things where you take the good with the bad. The lead police officer asked me to come in on the cases and help him lead the division on helping find this serial killer. I told them I would help them but I wouldn't lead the division. They said that was fair enough. When you consult with someone there is a price you have to pay. I didn't like consulting with them but they said they wanted someone that knew him. They had twenty unsolved cases in the town of what we called Black Death. The serial killer did the usual and it was just routine by now. It happened like that to every victim he killed and there were possibly more in other states. He may have traveled from other states. I called my brother and talked about the case.

I told him details about the two dimes on the eyes of the victims and he said that he had victims down in Florida that had two dimes on their eyes too. My brother was also a cop. He was a strong man that could take down a bull. He was the nicest guy with long wavy locks and he was going to make the ranks. He was one of the best in his division. He had one of the best crime solving rates in the county and it was mind boggling how good he was. My brother and I had similar interests, we both liked sports and we didn't have time for family with our jobs. We both put in long hours being dedicated to our jobs fighting crime.

There was a sketch of the serial killer, he had orange hair, a scar on his face. The witness was only alive long enough to give us the information. We put it in the papers and it was something to go off of finally. We didn't get any hits and the trail went cold. We figured he moved towns, stopped killing or moved states. He didn't just disappear. He stopped killing for three weeks and then he started again.

He killed a hooker and just like that it started

all over again and the cycle wasn't broken like we had thought. There was a certain comfort level you had to feel when you were killing to stop and start again. Killing wasn't in my blood but that didn't mean I didn't think about hurting the person that killed my son. It was something that I felt once before. They said she was a good earner and that the pimp thought she was top dollar whatever that meant. The pimp was a dick like the rest of them and he didn't really miss his bitch as he called her. To him she was just property and if you were a dead hooker you weren't earning anymore. That meant finding a new hooker to find to earn more money and that meant finding someone to take away from their family and prey upon them. This pimp always dressed flamboyantly and wore a fedora and he was always well dressed like he was a high class lawyer. Worrying about these girls was my job but finding this car was my top priority. To these pimps it was getting the girls on the streets and leaving them to the animals that hurt them week in and week out and the cops pay the price for it. We have to get the reports of rape and death and it sucks for us. With the serial killer leaving behind this big of clue we had to figure out how we were going to make this car ours and how we were going to find it. We had a sketch of a bad guy and a car that could be a lead that the hooker was taken in and possibly blood evidence in and if we had that we could nail him. We needed further details on where this car was and what this serial killer looked like. We had no needle in the haystack because there was no haystack. No one knew what this serial killer looked like because they didn't get a glimpse of him. We could hope for a confession from someone but that could be someone that wanted to be famous and that was something that we didn't want. There was nothing I could do but look at all the case files and see if there were any clues which I knew there weren't going to be any. There was nothing to go on and nothing I could sniff out. There was no light at the end of this tunnel and if there was we running towards it only to find out it was darkness with a train headed right towards us with a brick wall behind us. We couldn't escape the other way. There was just no hope and even if there was it was slim to none. We were up shit creek without a paddle and we had a rose petal in our minds keeping us moving forward. I think the killer was laughing at us. It was like sweet music to his ears. It was a showdown between man and wolf. We have had a black eye too many times so why do we keep trying to go another three rounds? It was time to look through this black eye and fight one last fight. It was time to take this bull down and win this fight. He had the knockout punch coming. There was no way to avoid death unless you took it head on told it you are ready and said come get me. I will take you down until there is nothing left of you but spirit mind and body. We were down for the count and all we knew that we were on our backs in the ring lying down until the count of ten. There was nothing holding us back besides this serial killer and ourselves. There was nothing to do but pout. We had our head in our hands crying wishing for better days. We had to wait until the next fight where we had no black eyes and no kidney punches. If better days were coming we needed the heart of a lion to survive. We came to win and the killer's heart was going to be in our hands. Until then we had to do old fashioned police work, rely on the forensics and just hope he left behind some DNA; a fingerprint or something to connect him to these crimes. Maybe something would come of this and get this guy caught. There had to be something that this sketch produced that would get someone to recognize him so we could catch him. There was no one that was this good at avoiding detection like this serial killer and we knew that better than anyone.

After forty people you think the police would catch him. After a serial killer gets comfortable there is a really slim chance of catching him. There is no way we are going to catch him if there's no evidence but we always relied on him slipping up and leaving something behind. There was one forensic files case on T.V. where a guy set seventy two fires and they caught him from a fingerprint and hypnosis. It got me thinking that this might work on our killer. There was something that said I didn't like that part of it and it was all here say and it was all what you could prove in court. My interest peaked when they showed the sketch of the serial killer. That was when I knew I was onto something.

Now it was showing the dead hooker but they didn't say what she did for a job they just said she was found on the streets. There was nothing wrong with that in my mind. No one needed to know her job because if they did they would say she wasn't a person; she was a hooker. Now it was a question of how many more people was he going to kill before we caught him. I was going to catch him with the task force working alongside me.

I got a call to be a bodyguard for a football player that said he was getting death threats from the twenty cent killer. I don't believe this was the twenty cent killer because this was way out of his comfort level and he would never threaten someone. He never warns people that he is going to kill them, he just does it. I asked how much the pay was and they said I was going to get paid ten thousand dollars if he made it out alive by the end of the week. That was fine with me and I wasn't going to protect him any longer than that. If they wanted any more protection than that they were going to have to have a squad car drive around the outside of his house. I was protecting the football player named John and there was an incident where his car got shot up and I knew it wasn't the killer. This was way out of my paygrade and in the end it was something that I wasn't qualified to do. He died a day later and it was something that was going to be in the news immediately. I didn't think that this killer had anything to do with this because it didn't smell like his kind of work with all the threats and all of that. There was something that said it was all about money and it was something that said family or friend. It was all done and I could go back to regular life behind the desk looking for the serial killer and making my life meaningful for once. He had killed the football player to try to kill me. He had done a miserable job. I think if he wanted me dead I would be dead. He was making a really interesting case of getting to know me and my family and really wanting to know what made me tick. There was nothing to suggest that the twenty cent killer was scared of me catching him. I think you should always take the chance of shooting and taking down the serial killer. I didn't think that he could hide from me forever and he was going to get caught for his murders.

I knew he had killed my brother but I wasn't about to go yell it all around the police force. I wasn't going to go tell anybody at home.

He was stabbing hookers twenty to thirty times which meant that he must have had a deep hatred for those type of women. The coroner was hoping that he wasn't going to kill all these hookers at once and scare them off. Hookers were thriving in this town and if they went away then most of them would go to another town and find something else.

Sex and money thrived and it was a sex driven town. People were always looking for a good time and if you take that away you take cheese off the pizza and they don't want the toppings anymore. All our evidence in the locker had gotten tossed away because it was deemed useless. No one was coming forward. The serial killer was taunting us. We don't think that his face had changed after three years but one never knows. I think people were just scared that he was going to kill them at any moment. There was going to be a nice time to get a break in the case and get some new leads if they ever came in. There was going to be a time when this serial killer was a distant memory in our past. He was going to wreak havoc in the hearts and minds of the people we have come to know and love. He had killed so many people and taken all they had worked hard for. People were being taken from their homes and their families. There was no reason for murdering them but he did it anyway. When you kill someone you run the risk of getting caught. The people will become the law if you let them report anything they think is suspicious. They will listen to the police radio and turn in anybody for nothing. There is always a jail cell waiting for the next contestant. People will find out that jail and prison aren't just three meals a day, playing cards, rec time and working out. You have to fight your way to the top and if you don't fight with the people in your gang you will soon find out you get shanked and raped and the hole isn't the worst thing that happens to you. This killer doesn't just have fans. He has followers and dedicated bloggers following him to make sure he will always live on. There is a killer in all of us and I didn't know who was going to be the next killer walking the streets. They are so dedicated that they make you think they are killers too. There were also people that would want to find this serial killer and take the law into their own hands. They wanted to make sure there was something they could do to see that this serial killer died. I wanted to save this town like any other cop but no one wanted to help me. I want to be a movie buff and spend all my time watching the best movies. I want to make all my time about movies. I love movies and some of them are so classic that I want to watch them over and over. I get the best use out of them by watching them five or six times in a row. I wanted this serial killer to know I was hot on his trail. I wanted him to know he was on the top of my list to hunt down and kill. It takes a lot of hard work to become a serial killer because you have to have a stomach for blood and you have to have a killing style. The flip side of that is it's hard to catch a serial killer because you need to get in the mind of a serial killer. Sometimes you want to become that serial killer. When thinking like a serial killer you have to ask: what is his next move? Who is he going to kill next and why is he killing these people? It was going to be no sleep and all-nighters. All-nighters and coffee is what cops lived for and that was what made a cop stronger like a bull in a desert. There was nothing I couldn't do if I set my mind to it. There was nothing I was doing that I wouldn't do differently if I thought about it. I knew the serial killer was thinking the same way. This serial killer was good and I would have said I was better but he was winning every battle like a chess game. Chess is a game of knowledge and logic and if you are going to beat your opponent you are going to do counter moves and shadowing.

Two people killed was too much because one was just bound to happen but the second kill meant you made a mistake and you weren't willing to admit it. That was a given and that was why you were give that task, to catch him after the first kill. There was going to be no justice there was just going to be peace throughout this town. Justice always prevailed over evil every time and sometimes justice just needed to be served by a good hand that was guided by God. There was only so much you could do sometimes.

Now I was looking at another murder because the twenty cent serial killer struck again. We were still keeping the twenty cents over the eyes out of the papers and it was something that was going to stay out of the papers for the remainder of the time. There was no time to spend telling the media that there was a major clue that a copy cat killer could mimic. It would be a shit storm that no one would want to deal with. It would be a lot of work finding the real serial killer and that was why we left it out of the paper. There was nothing that I wanted more than to know who this serial killer was.

The serial killer had killed a basketball player from high school. He had been playing since seventh grade. Since seventh grade he had scored a thirty points in one game. He was murdered in the gym. The gym was closed off and there was a blood pool on the floor. There was nothing to suggest that it was anyone that had witnessed the killing. It was a bust that way but they had seen a suspicious car driving around the parking lot. They said it was a sixty seven mustang. It was a beautiful car and I wanted it to say that at the least but I couldn't afford it. This guy was driving a nice car, dressed in fancy clothes, was clean cut and clean shaven. He wore cologne and he had an expensive haircut. He was wearing sunglasses with brown hair and a black beard. That was all they knew. That was very helpful and it was just like they knew everything. They said he didn't have car. That was weird to me and must have been something that was getting to all the cops that were working on the case.

I went home and sensed somebody was there. I got stabbed three times with a deep laceration and a broken arm. I shot him and that was the end of it. There was a through and through gunshot to the killer and I knew I had to be a better shot if he was going to be checked into the hospital. There was pain but it would have been more pain if I was going to make something out of who the serial killer was. It was the twenty cent killer and I didn't know who would have the balls to do this. There was nothing that was making sense anymore and it was all about routine. It was all about who had the routine down and who was making their routine different from everyone else. I was so close to finding something useful in this case and the serial killer knows where I live. How does the serial killer know where I live? There was going to be a good hunt when I opened another investigation into what kind of gun was used in the shooting of the high school basketball player.

There was another kill and this kill wasn't any different because he was dead and no amount of grieving could bring him back. There were going to be cases that were going to be related and then there were going to be cases that were going to be random. There was nothing that was a coincidence but there were things that were related in some way or another. Sometimes these kills made me think there was a higher power at work. I didn't know why I thought that. These were what connected these kills and what made these kills special. Everything was going to fall into place in the end and that I was what I was confident in. There was nothing that made sense in these murders anymore because they were random. Everything was a thrill until he got caught or was dead. There was nothing that was making the killer stop, not even that there was a sketch of him. We weren't going to arrest him anytime soon so that meant he was going to kill forever it seemed. The arrest of this serial killer was going to mean that he couldn't kill any more people and ruin any more lives. It was going to put away a guy that was on the loose wreaking havoc. It was time to follow up on some tips that people had called in on. I followed every tip and it was good that they were calling in. Most of the tips were useless and they were going nowhere. When he took a break from killing everybody wondered why. It was like we needed something new to scare him out of his fox hole. We weren't going to scare him. It was something that we needed to do to put him on the ropes once again. My wife was still in a depression over our son's murder. She had been taking pills but they weren't helping. I told her not to stop taking the pills and talk to the doctor about new pills but she refused.

I came home to her suicide one night and that was the final straw. I knew I hadn't helped her one bit and the truth was there was nothing I could have done. There was something that said she would have committed suicide with or without the pills. They didn't let me see her body on the floor when I got into the house. They wheeled her out of the house and let me see her body on the metal slide out table only for identification. She was peaceful and I thought there was nothing better than her being in a peaceful place. There was nothing that was going to happen that I wasn't prepared for. There was something that said I needed to set flowers on her grave every day to remember how great she was.

Losing my wife and my son was tragic. I knew I would never find anyone like them again. I knew there was no one to replace such great people in my life. I took ten minutes to talk to my son and it was something that made me feel at home once again. It was a family reunion and I knew I would be resting with them again. There was nothing I had left now that the serial killer had not already taken away from me. Come take what I had already lost and make me what I am. What is taken cannot be lost and a flower cannot be dead but will be reborn into a delicate pedal going to the path of a destination unknown. What we have left behind will not be forgotten but will always be in the future of our generations. There was nothing that was left undone until the hands were washed clean. The serial killer clearly stole what was mine and I was going to get it back. Now that there was something missing from my life it was a dream in reality.

This is a reality I will live every day and if I am lucky I can die a sweet dream away from this cruel world. With my wife killing herself it raised many questions saying why did this happen and if this was a reality in my life how long was I going to drink to make this depression go away? The sad reality was even thought the killer took her away from me the killer wasn't at fault here. It was my fault for letting it go on this long. There was nothing to do but make things worse and get my ego involved and get more cops involved in my wife's murder. There was going to be nothing left to chance. There was nothing that was going to make me think that this serial killer knew any of my pain. I got a tip that was useful and that made me go on a trip to another county. It made me think that the serial killer was killing in another county but it was a false lead. There was a break in and we responded immediately. It was near an apartment that was run down and it was going to be a good bust. There was a guy we spotted breaking in and we arrested him. He was brought into custody and put in a jail cell.

There was another kill in a rough part of town and it was just the right time in winter where it wasn't too cold. It was fifty degrees and the body was face down with a large shotgun blast to the back of the head. He was missing part of his head and it was brain matter on the ground. It was something I had seen before. There was something that said it was all too familiar. There was something that said I didn't like this.

He had sped off and it was like he wanted to be chased. If he would have been driving casually there would have been no suspicion on him. For how sloppy the crime scene was there were no prints on the rifle. It was something that we had come to expect. We couldn't nail him to anything and it was like it was the cleanest mess we had ever seen. If there was an award for being the most cleanly kill on the messiest street he would win. It was the ghetto and he could have pinned it on anyone. The killer we had put away had told someone what he had put two dimes on the eyelids and it was a shame that there was something that he had done wrong. There was nothing we could have done different.

We had put away a construction worker but something didn't feel right. Some of the other construction workers felt that he had done it until he had given the confession. They read the papers and they knew the details. They knew what wasn't in the papers and they were smart. This was a shut down case for some but not me. there was something that said this wasn't the guy. This was a copycat kill in and out and we had to find this killer. There were other serial killers confessed to these types of crimes. there he was killing going about his day and people would emulate him. Everyone strived to be him and the sad truth was they couldn't kill like him. There was no one like him even if they had his killing style. I had to assume that there were going to be bullet casings behind and that was just a theory. I wanted some evidence before I went crazy. The cat was going to eat the mouse eventually unless it was a Tom and Jerry situation. There is always a time for zero mistakes but this is not a time for that. I need something that is going to wake me up. All this serial killer knows is random and secrecy in the world. It seems that there is nothing more than a killer instinct and a dedication for more. I feel the days of a car at the crime scene is over but that is just my opinion. I needed to think he was just taunting us at that moment. I put the wrong serial killer away and I knew that I had done wrong. It seemed there was nothing I could do right. There was something about this that seemed odd. It was something that was going to haunt me. The police want me to share details but I am not about to share my evidence with the FBI. It is give up and share everything or get in trouble and go on suspension. I shared everything when I needed to. there were no more copycats and I was happy about that. If you were going to kill be original and think about what you were going to do. You should know how you were going to come up with a killing style. The twenty cents killer was original and it was something that was clever. It was something that I respected as a cop even though I hated him. Even with the copycat killer behind bars I had clipped the feathers of the dove. The peace was out of the town because there was only one serial killer in the town. I thought that the natural balance out of order. His feathers were beautiful but he was just another peacock. There was nothing to do but catch him, end my career and go back to work at Wal-Mart. Wal-Mart was my true calling not this private investigator business because I was too old and slow. This Wal-Mart business was the life for me. You take your time, no one bothers you and you help our customers. You also get to work at your own pace. It takes you to a different place. Your world is your paradise. There is nothing that makes you go nuts like a serial killer killing. He kills a whole bunch of people and you cant do a darn thing. There is nothing you can do when a killer moves freely from place to place like a drifter. He moves through the wind like sand over the beach.

All these people dead on your doorstep with blood on your hands was something that you will think about forever. The killing gets to your head and you think who is he going to kill next? You hope that he stops with a smile on his face and the beach under his feet. The beach sounds good with a pina colada in my hands and a Jack Daniels in my stomach for another day spent at my home.

There was another kill and it was a skateboarder and I felt like if he was smashed over the head that would be a good day. There was something that said I needed that to happen. All the skateboarders would realize how stupid they looked doing it and how stupid and fake the sport was. There were so many things that were wrong with the sport that I couldn't explain them all. There were no police to work on this so we moved onto the next case.

We werent even looking at this case because this next kill happened the next day.

We were doing drug busts and shutting down meth labs. The shootouts were happening weekly. It seemed that it was happening routinely and it was all great until you got into that situation. Anyone that said they weren't scared to pull their gun was a liar.

The scariest call to get called into is a domestic dispute because they are arguing with each other. They can turn on you and pull a weapon and kill you just as fast. It was all a jumbled mess and it was all the calls that made it unbearable. It was something that was going to make me think what was it all for? There were hookers, drug dealers and cops all in it together. There was a cop that was forty and he looked fifty with graying hair.

He had no time to draw his gun at that age because he was too old and slow. With his hand on the trigger he was dead and he was called quick trigger but not this time. It was a joke because he was so slow at pulling his gun. He had no chance and he was on the call by himself. I felt bad and it was supposed to be his partner but he died in a shootout. They didn't have enough cops. He was a seasoned vet that didn't have a chance. I felt bad for him but if he was given a chance to have a partner at his side this wouldn't have happened. There was a chance that this was a female serial killer we were dealing with because there was a hint of perfume in the apartment. We figured if the apartment smelled like perfume it must be a female serial killer. There was nothing that was going that was going that wasn't beyond my reach. There was something that was troubling me, this seemed like it was a girl serial killer because of the hint of perfume in the apartment. I had to be wrong because there weren't that many woman serial killers. There weren't that many female serial killers. There were serial killers in the past that had been woman. I could just feel for these families and what they were going through. There was nothing that was going to surprise me but this could surprise me because this could be his daughter. There wasn't much that shocked me but losing someone like my kid is something that shocked me. I never thought it would happen to me. Not that it was a girl but that it could be a daughter of the serial killer or something like that. There was a seriousness about this serial killer. When this serial killer killed he didn't mess around. it was one quick kill and it was done. Either he was a fast runner or he could drive away without anyone noticing a car. With the other serial killer I sensed that he had stuck around for the cops at the crime scene. I watched them investigate the crime scene even though it was a bad idea. He stuck around when it was crowded and it was a seriousness with this new serial killer. I was sensing that there was going to be nothing left to chance. There were going to be a lot of duplicate kills. Too many of these kills were going to be duplicates and it was going to be a mistake. It was going to be a mistake on the killer's part because we could warn the cops. The basketball players and the hookers would get some security to protect them. There was going to be an extra eye on the people that were going to be the next targets. They knew they were going to be next.

With the hookers it looked like the killer was getting the hookers into the car, driving them to a secluded spot, killing them, and dumping them under a bridge. There was a certain calmness you had to have when killing. When we caught the first serial killer we got lucky and it was a good thing going for us. There was a serial killer on the loose and we had to find him before the death count got too high and people started killing innocent people. We didn't want people taking justice into their own hands and start killing innocent people. There were going to be more people that this serial killer was going to kill and it was going to be more random people.

I got a call about four in the morning about a sportscaster being shot and falling off a ten story building. It was a long fall and we knew it was the twenty cent killer. The fall killed him because he was shot in the arm and he had fallen off the roof. He was probably forced up onto the roof and up to the edge. He fell ten stories and it a tragedy. There was nothing that could have been done to prevent this. It was safe to say they didn't know each other. There was nothing to suggest that this was anything but a shot to the arm and a simple fall. The door had locked at the top. The killer had to have put something in the door to hold it open. There was nothing around that would suggest that it was used to prop open the door. The sportscaster was very good at her job and interviewed many people. She was the best person to do her job. She had interviewed Kevin Love, LeBron James and James Hardon. There were a few people on her resume she had interviewed at her job that made her look like she had been doing it her whole life. She was the best and the sports world was going to miss her. She was good and she was going to leave a legacy behind her. She was going to have people emulating her and imitating her. It was going to go that way and there were going to be people that were going to interview people that she interviewed. There were people asking them questions that she had asked them. It was going to be because she had set the standard for that. She had left a legacy and nothing was going to change that. Her memories would live on and I would always have her pictures as a reminder of what a good person she was. I had pictures of her moments before she died and that was a comfort for me. There was nothing that comforted me more than that. I wanted her back more than you could ever know. I was hitting a wall trying to figure out who could have killed her and there were no leads. I drank to forget and there was nothing to do but find the twenty cent serial killer.

The serial killer had recently killed a kid riding a skateboard and it was in the middle of the street. There was nothing that made sense because he was killing a variety of different people. I didn't know how he was selecting his victims or how he was selecting them. This was a high traffic road but there was no traffic at this time of day. It was weird because it was like the kills were exciting the serial killer. It didn't seem like the serial killer got nervous when he was killing. He didn't seem to care about the police when he was killing. The police couldn't catch him and there were no signs of him slowing down. There was no signs of him going to different counties. It seemed like he was choosing the same three mile radius. We were wondering if he was close to where these murders took place or if just wanted us to think so. He had us chasing our tails. We wanted him to stop but so we could investigate the case files. We figured he was going to kill at least one person a day. There was nothing I wanted more than to catch him but I wasn't going to catch him anytime soon. We all had demons and our demons were going to come out. If we could get them to rest then they were going to go to hell. There were good serial killers and there were great serial killers. I was dealing with a great serial killer. He had the urge to kill and maybe if we stopped that urge we could catch him. I needed to do old fashioned police work and not let the mayhem of this town get to me. We had nothing to work with but that didn't mean we had to give up. We had no fingerprints, footprints nothing that would tie anyone to this crime. There was nothing that I was missing because there was nothing at the crime scenes. I was stumped and I asked myself how I could move this case along. I asked some of the seasoned cops to help me and they were just as stumped as I was. We looked over the cases and we didn't find anything. This was just one big headache and we were thinking that there was no hope.

We found one bullet casing at a crime scene that a cop threw away in a trash can. The cop retired and we asked him why he threw it away. He said he was paid a certain amount of money but he wasn't giving a name. He was dead the next day and we knew it was the serial killer. That was our biggest lead. We thought we would get something from examining the bullet but that wasn't the case. We knew it was the Browning .22 pistol and we knew we had something. We got even more excited when the expert confirmed our results. I was watching sports center when I got a call and it was urgent.

There was a good kill at our hands and it wasn't supposed to reach the papers. There was something off about this serial killer, suddenly he was killing celebrities. It didn't make sense and I for one didn't want to be in a world where a serial killer wanted attention in the papers. I wasn't going to give him the attention he thought he deserved. He was going to be in the papers for a different reason. There was information in the paper that a gun was found. Another Browning was found and it seemed to be another gun that was being copied by other serial killer. I had a feeling that these serial killers wanted to be like him in every way and I didn't like copycat killers. I wanted them to have their killing style and not rip off someone else. In the end we had our hands full with one serial killer so why were we focusing on copycat killers? We could get lucky and he could taunt us. He was going to leave something behind and I could become closer to him in some way.

I wanted to get inside his head. I wanted to be like him in the fact that I didn't care about anything in my life. I was watching Netflix on my computer and it was just another time where it was a good forensic files. I wanted to catch this serial killer more than anyone. I knew I could spend the rest of my life hunting him and searching for evidence but I also knew he was elusive so it was a game of trickery. The only thing that was left behind wasn't going to hold up in court. I knew I needed something more. The more evidence I had the better and I knew there was something more I could do. There was more in these case files and all we had to do is find it. So we kept looking hoping there was something we missed.

There was another hooker killed in a hotel this time and it was suspected that there was sex involved. There was no physical evidence found but we weren't going to give up hope. No one saw them come in which meant they weren't willing to talk. That was the worst thing to happen to the case. He was a stranger on a train talking to everyone. He wasn't shy to killing. We still thought this serial killer was a woman. She thought she was throwing us off by purchasing a hooker. She just ordered a room to taunt us. Kill someone in plain sight and make sure you scare the living daylights out of the whole town. We were looking down all the dark alleys but soon enough the leads were going to die off. Catching him now wasn't necessary a good thing unless we killed him. if we killed him there was no paper work. There was nothing we could do but sit on our hands and go about our business. We could wait for him to kill someone and leave behind the forensic evidence but why wait for that when we knew he wasn't going to leave anything else behind? We had what we needed we just needed a fingerprint or something. That wasn't going to happen anytime soon and I was going to wait for that day and hope for it to come. That was a day that I was going to wait for because he was too good and we didn't have enough seasoned cops. There were a lot of people in the police force that wanted him caught but why catch him when we could kill him? It was less paperwork and we could get his demons out in the open. It was going to prevent him from gaining any followers. There was a pain in my side and a sour taste in my mouth from chasing him for so long. There were a lot of people dying at his hands and his thirst for blood was infinite. He was just getting started and I was afraid for my life. I think he knew everyone's secret fear and it was something he fed on. It was something that I could work on.

There was something that said I had demons and I needed to work them out. There was nothing that I was doing to show that I was getting any closer to solving these cases. He was too good and he was always a step ahead of me. He had a comfort zone that he was in and we had to break him of that if we were ever going to catch him. There was a sickness he had to have to kill all of these people and he was holding their lives in his hands. Their lives were snatched away and they were bait to bigger fish. I had no idea of who he was or how to catch him. The trick was how to identify him without any eye witnesses at the hotel. With no help from the front desk at the hotel and no help from the bullet we had nothing. Nothing was coming together and the cases were turning cold fast.

The next week a T.V. reporter was murdered. She was testifying against a key murderer in a key trial. They said it was the trial of the century. We needed her and she was reporting out in the field and in front of the camera. She was all over the place and she was getting paid well. Now it was getting personal for him and he was just doing this for fun. He was killing big time people and she was someone that grew up in this town. He was taunting us saying catch me if you can. We needed to set up a trap and make him afraid of us. There was nothing in this case that surprised me about these cases. This world wasn't for me and if I left was anyone going to care? There was no way we could catch this serial killer because he was too good. He enjoyed the attention of the papers and the mayhem of the town made him salivate. He was a great serial killer that we couldn't catch. He was enjoying putting these cops on their toes and making us look like fools. This was going to be the best case of my career and it was going to define my life. It was going to define everything I had worked for and I needed this to boost my confidence. Nothing else mattered to me. I was going to be the hero and then I was going to retire on a god note. I had a specialty and that was catching people. Putting them away was my life. I loved sitting in my boat fishing. I could be catching fish and drinking beer in Mexico but that was just a dream. It was relaxing to me and I loved every minute of it reeling in the fish and eating them at home. There was some good fishing out there and I knew where they were. Now it was time to figure out where the serial killer was going to hit next.

He burnt down a church next and it was nothing new. He had burnt down three churches before and it was something that was in the news three months ago and it was the first story on the news. I was baffled it was a Christian church. There was nothing that was going to right now that the church burnt down.

The next thing that happened that was wrong, was an orphanage blowing up with thirty kids and three adults in it. This was serious and the body count was up to four hundred and seventy three.

There was nothing that that was out of his comfort zone after this kill. His comfort zone was very high and we knew he was going to keep escalating. We also knew that he was just going to keep getting bolder. He was all about killing whoever he wanted and he was killing whoever he wanted and being random. He had never used a bomb to blow up an orphanage before. I didn't know that he knew how to build a bomb. It shows how much I knew about his skills and his capabilities. This serial killer knew a lot of things and it was safe to say that it was going to be a long time before we caught him.

He killed a gas station employee and took the money out of the cash register. It wasn't like him. It was only 373 dollars in the cash register. He showed he would do whatever he wanted. There were no fingerprints at the crime scene. Gloves were used and we knew that this was a professional killer. He was killing a lot of people and there were so many people per day that we couldn't fathom. It was a low risk high reward when he was killing. There was a bank robbery and it wasn't our serial killer. There was nothing we could go on. There was nothing that was going on this time that was getting us to think he would take this much of a risk to get caught. We caught the bank robber and recovered the stolen cash. They had insurance but we returned it to the bank anyways. The bank was thankful and I was happy. I was going to make the serial killer pay for all of his crimes. I was going to make his crimes stick to him. I was going in circles with these crimes. It was safe to say the bombs had no fingerprints on them. The bombs were homemade and they were filled with nails and gunpowder. There were a few other ingredients and it was safe to say he had done this before. There was nothing I wanted to do other than bring those kids back. They could have been adopted by families and as far as I knew that was the only orphanage in town. It was a shame and I wanted those kids to have a family. All I wanted was for those kids to get adopted and now that wasn't in their futures. If my brother was here he would have known what to do. He would have thought up a plan to build another orphanage. There was a call about an intruder and we rushed over because our first thought was the serial killer. I was mad that the signs didn't point to the serial killer. It was something that I needed to figure out. I had to realize that the serial killer didn't do break-ins. I was watching forensic files on Netflix when I got a call that the intruder had been caught. He had stabbed someone else. He matched a description someone else had given the police. That was case closed and he went to jail for both stabbings. I was happy and it was the news I had been waiting for a year. There was no bigger relief for me than this news that I had gotten a few minutes ago. Now that I had gotten the news I slept like a baby that night. I couldn't express how happy I was.

I was at home sleeping when I was called to

the scene of a journalist who had been shot in the head. He had fallen from the third floor. It was a messy scene and there was blood splattered all over the cement. Some would say it was like paint had been thrown all over the crime scene. There was something that was wrong with this crime scene. There was no struggle which meant the victim knew the killer or was taken by surprise. Maybe the killer took him by surprise or maybe he knew how to kill him without a struggle. We didn't find any drugs in the system so that meant he was probably taken by surprise. It was something that we had to go off of. I didn't know what was going on. All I knew is I was in a great depression after my son died and I had been drinking ever since. I was doing drugs and my family knew it. That was the only way I could escape the fate of not catching this serial killer. I was spending all my free time at the strip clubs. That was the only place I could hide out in the dark depths of hell so no one could find me. It was the place to hang your hat and give up. I was starting to give up on these cases. It was sad to say that these families didnt have any cops that cared if the cases were solved. There was nothing I could do but give up and drink myself to death.

My niece was trying to save me from myself but she couldn't. No one could save me from the darkness that was the life that I had chosen for myself. I didn't want to get out of this pit of misery. It was all a matter of time before the walls came crumbling down and my empire fell. The only way to cope was to make everyone feel sorry for me. I wanted to make the world hate me as much as I hated myself. Now it was time to give up and let this case take on a new life. Let someone take this case on and make this case their own burden.

I got in my car and started driving fast and reckless not caring about what was in front of me. I was driving a 64 mustang and it was in great condition. I saw my life flash before my eyes and then I was in heaven for a couple of seconds. I didn't know where I was going but I knew where I had been. I figured if I lived my whole life on the edge someone would notice me and try to help me. I was lucky to be in a coma with a few broken ribs and a broken pelvis. Now it was time to rebuild my car and get it in running shape again. I was willing to pay any price for happiness and money didn't matter to me. I got a large inheritance from my dad and that was about thirty million because he was a great business man. He was a real estate investor and he loved to buy houses fix them up and sell them. He sold them for a big profit and I was always amazed. Our dad was also an author. He was a New York times best seller fourteen times and it was so amazing what he could accomplish. He had his demons, like drinking himself to death and doing drugs in his later years. In the end he was a great father and making his millions didn't change him. That was the dark side to him and his demons controlled him like all of us. When his demons came out everyone in our family paid the price because he beat the crap out of my brother and me. It was a side to him we had seen many times. It came out about once a week. He had raped our mom on more than one occasion. She hid the scars and bruises for years. She was getting beaten up on numerous occasions because he had a violent temper. He would throw things and it would hit my mom in the shoulder and I remember it breaking her arm. It was a side of him that we saw all too often and I didn't want to be around him when he was this way. It would become screaming matches and if you stood up to him you would get hit. I remember my first black eye when I was eleven and I knew that I didn't want to make him mad. It was like a tornado hit a volcano. There was a force that would hit an immovable force but eventually it would take pieces of you and destroy you. There was nothing my dad wouldn't say to make you feel like you were nothing. There was a kinder side to him that no one knew. It was something that made want to stay. Then there were times where you just wanted to kill him. There was a time where he twisted my mom's arm out of her socket and I had to drive her to the E.R. My dad went to work three hours later like nothing had happened and I needed him to know what he had done. He was tearing this family apart one piece at a time and I didn't think it was right. I was mad about everything as a kid but that didn't mean I didn't have a happy life. There was nothing about my dad that was good that I could think of growing up. Maybe if I told him to stop drinking things would have been different. The bad times were the only times I could think of now and that was sad to me. The bad times were the only times that mattered when I talked about my dad. My dad was a wife beating piece of shit and that was how I chose to remember him. There was nothing good about him except when he helped us with our homework. We always got perfect homework and we always studied well with my dad. I never understood why he beat my mom. I think it was for the simple fact that it was in his head that he could get away with it. The only thing that set him off was beer and being told no. He was dead by the time he was fifty and that meant no more beating and no more drinking. It also meant no more fighting about nothing. There was someone for everyone and she had found her someone. There was always going to be those bad memories and those were the memories I would carry around with me until I die.

I had been in the hospital with overdoses as a teenager huffing a cleaner by accident. It was a mistake staying up for a couple of weeks straight and it was hell. I was so strung out I couldn't eat, I couldn't sleep, I couldn't shower, I smelled and everyone noticed. It was all my own personal hell. It was all downhill in the hospital and I sued them and got two million dollars. It was a gravy train. I saved up and I put it all on bonds to be used later down the road. I was just a rich teenager and I used it to get into forensics and then I became a cop for twenty years and retired because I was tired of getting shot at. There were so many bullets flying and I was tired of it and now I was a cop again. It was a job that was disappointing knowing I couldn't catch a serial killer that was smarter than I was. There was nothing that was going to catch him if there was no forensics. There was no old fashioned police work that was going to catch him. There was going to have to be forensic evidence to catch him and there was none. There was nothing that we had to catch him and that's why I was doing drugs and drinking in excess. There was nothing better than drugs because I was finally happy. I was so depressed and there was nothing that was going to make me happy. I was just so depressed that I couldn't find motivation to leave my apartment. Now it was time to try and look at these cases and the shell casings in the victim's heads. They looked like a thirty eight pistol. No gun is the same, you look at the rifling inside the gun and that is how each gun is different. There were thousands of these guns out there and we were never going to find this gun unless we had a victim to ask him where it was. There was nothing that was going to make this case easy. We knew this case was going to be hard to solve without that key piece of evidence. We had nothing and the killer knew it. He continued to kill and he was in his comfort zone. He was killing while we were chasing our tails looking for him. I was starting to give up on these cases going through a bottle of Jack Daniels every week. It was just getting way too expensive to drink so I cut back and I was getting paid well. I was going to get into a greater depression if I kept drinking. It was going to be even more depressing and it was going to take a toll on me. I was doing three lines of cocaine a day and it was expensive. I was blowing through my inheritance and I stopped altogether. I was going to get through this. I was going to solve this case and we were going to bring this serial killer down. No one was going to laugh at us after we caught this serial killer. There was going to be no fun for him when he stopped killing. He was going to be caught when we found his gun. There was going to be fun for us when we caught him. There was going to be a sense of pride when we caught him. We were going to catch him before he stopped killing if he stopped. I had a feeling he would never stop because he wouldn't ever caught. There were going to be a fingerprint or something eventually. I was going to make sure he screwed up. I was going to be at the crime scene to investigate everything it had to offer. There was going to be nothing to make me think that there was anything mentally wrong with this serial killer. There was something I was missing with these crime scene photos. I was overlooking something. I was missing an important clue somewhere. I needed a sense of closure with this case. I needed to solve this case soon otherwise I was going to go crazy. I needed this case to be solved because he was better than me. If I solved this maybe I could get redemption for my brother. We pulled one over on this serial killer. That meant we were better than him at that particular moment. This was just the thing we needed to solve this case. We had good forensic evidence and good cops willing to put their lives on the line. They needed to put their guns on the serial killer and kill him if need be. Put the case away and save that next victim. There was a sense of urgency to save that next victim if we could. We knew we wouldn't because we couldn't. We never knew the targets and we never knew how he picked them. Now he was moving to Ravens edge the town next to Ravensdale. We moved with him and we continued to track his movements.

It was just another case of getting into more politics and since he killed a mayor. There was high alert on white house officials. He was killed at his house in Washington and he had driven past the security.

The next kill was a senator and everybody was losing their minds. It was anarchy and there was nothing I could do because no one knew who did it. There was nothing that I could do and I felt helpless. Now the white house was on high alert. With the white house it was the president that was going to make sure that this wasn't going to happen again.

There was nothing more dangerous than someone killing white house officials. It was awful and I was just flabbergasted. I couldn't find the words to describe how mad I was. Now it was time to get down to business and find out who this serial killer was. There was no way we were going to find him until he left something behind. He never left anything behind and it was something that he was good at. There was something everyone was good at and he was good at killing. There was wine at my doorstep and I tested it in the lab and I found nothing wrong with it and I dumped it out. I was suspicious of who sent it and I found no fingerprints on it. I found no letter or anything and I saw no one coming by the house the last couple of days. I kept my eyes wide open and knew it was the serial killer. I hadn't been keeping that close of an eye on our neighborhood and I was just skeptical of what was in that bottle. It could have been something untraceable. There were things that broke down in liquids and it was just suspicious. I was still wondering who left the wine on my doorstep. There was a possibility that the killer had left it to poison me. Someone wanted me to drink it and thought that I was stupid. After all these kills he left it now and it was weird. It was going to be the worst trick in the book. If he wanted to kill me than he should have just shot me in the head and got it over with. Maybe he didn't want me dead. Maybe it was just a neighbor for a good deed or something. I was just taking safety measures by dumping out the wine just in case the serial killer had sent it. There was nothing that was going to kill me including the wine. I wanted to drink that wine but it was risky. I wasn't going to take any chances. The chances that the wine was poisoned was slim to none but I wasn't going to take any chances. Now that I was seeing all these kills taking place it was like second nature. It was horrible to think that the families had to live without one less family member. There was nothing that I liked more than my police work but this serial killer was rattling my cage. I couldn't wrap my head around the fact that he was killing everyone with no witnesses. There were so many families losing a family member. There was no one that was seeing this serial killer for who he was, a monster with a dark soul.

They were afraid that he was using a lock pick to break in and killing his victims. He was good enough to get out and use a silenced pistol. He was just toying with our division. I had caught many serial killers as a cop but they had left behind evidence. We could catch him and I knew that I needed to have some confidence if I was going to catch him. I was a good cop ten years ago but those were the glory years and I didn't want to remember those years. I was losing patience and I was going to give up soon if I didn't find him. There was nothing I could do to catch him and it was pissing me off. I was drinking my problems away in my mind. I thought it was helping to a certain extent but after a while it was getting old. I was getting drunk every day and knowing I was killing my liver was a problem. I was getting to the point where I was a filthy drunk. Every day was a drinking day and I wasn't enjoying it anymore. It was never fun and no one could save me from myself. My brother would have known I was a drunk and he couldn't tell me not to drink anymore. There was nothing to do but drink and forget this serial killer. He was going to kill one of my family members and he was going to do it soon. I had to try and stop him but without knowing which one he was going to kill I was helpless. If I could figure out which one he was going to kill I could foil his plan and then he would give up altogether. He was going to kill someone I loved and I was going to have to speak at another funeral. There was nothing I could say to bring any one of my family members back. That was the cold hard truth. The truth was that I didn't get to see much of my family members much anymore because they were all too far away. They were all across the state and they wanted me to sober up. I wasn't ready to sober up because that wasn't me. I was too busy drinking and trying to find this serial killer. I vowed that I would stop drinking and doing drugs until I found this serial killer. There was nothing more important than finding this serial killer and if he killed my family it meant that it would fuel me to find him. It was going to make me mad and make me want to find him more. It was going to add fuel to the fire. It was going to drive me to find him and it was going to make it personal for me.

He was killing hookers left and right along with porn stars and models. He was just getting a thrill out of killing these kind of people. I don't know how he was finding these porn stars and models. He was just getting a sexual thrill by assaulting them and it was all a game to him. He never left his DNA behind and that was smart because then we had nothing to compare it to. There was nothing we could do but sit on our hands and hope to get lucky with the next kill. There was nothing that made us get into the groove. We were never going to get any further in these cases at this slow of pace. There was nothing that made us get into the case more than music, donuts and coffee. We got the crime scene photos together and spent some time at all the crime scenes and we made some progress.

They all took place within a ten year span and it was all worth about ten thousand kills. He was killing two people a day and he was becoming more dangerous. He was upping his game and the bodies were hitting the floor. There were no real links between his kills. It was safe to say there was something to be questioned about these crimes. The first question was why was he killing so many hookers? Did he have a special hatred for hookers, porn stars and strippers? Did he all of a sudden have to kill two people a day to make our work harder? Now he was dangerous again and he was just making our work harder. He was going to make us get up earlier to investigate these killings. These killings weren't related besides killing the same types of people.

Next he killed a college baseball player and he was good too. He pitched a shutout game yesterday in nine innings and it was a good game. He had a 2.19 ERA last season and that was the best in baseball. There was nothing better than a good pitcher on a good team. They made the playoffs last year and beat two teams. They lost but their fan base increased by ten percent. It was a good thing too because there was a lot of people at the games last year. They had affordable ticket prices and I had been to the games. They were always close and they always pitched shutouts. I was going to most of the games just to watch this young pitcher. He would throw 95 mile an hour fast balls. He would throw great curve balls that would get the batter looking at his feet. There was nothing more fun to watch than this pitcher and his sinker. He was the best in baseball for a reason. I was impressed and he would have went in the first round next year if he wouldn't have been killed. It was sad he had been killed but God takes you when it's your time. It was just his time and I went to the funeral as did hundreds of fans. There were hundreds of fans there for support and giving money as sympathy and to raise money. The cards were filled with thoughts and memories of his games. He was a great family man and always put his family first. There was a charity event and it was more like a fund raiser. There was a memorial the next week and that was why they held the charity. It raised $20,000. That was astonishing and I was so happy that I shook their hands and gave my condolences. I gave them a card and it was a sympathy card so it was something I felt was right.

I was going to be going to a funeral of one of my family members and I was blamed for my niece's death. I didn't protect her and that was my biggest regret. They blamed me for her death and they were dead to me. They didn't want to talk to me and I and I felt the same. I would always have love in my heart for them. It would take me a long time for me to get rid of that grudge. There was nothing I had to say to my family about my niece's death that wasn't said already. They were just mad I didn't stop the serial killer from killing my niece. I didn't know who the serial killer was so how could I stop him? There was something so wrong that made me sick to my stomach when I saw the crime scene of my niece. She was stabbed at the crime scene not shot like all the others. There was nothing she would have said to me in that phone call that would have made me feel any better before her death. There was nothing in that phone call that made me feel comforted when my brother called me that could have soothed me. He told me who could have killed him. With all the people that had been killed there had been no neighbors that had seen the car that drove off with the serial killer in it. I found that weird and I also found it weird that he stabbed my brother. He usually shot his victims and now he stabbed my brother. It didn't make sense and now it was personal. It made me want to find this serial killer even more. When someone you love gets killed and you are asked to investigate the crime it is hard not to want to kill the guy who did it. I know I wanted to kill him and there was going to be a time when I was going to catch him. When I caught him I was going to get him to confess to me. The evidence was going to put him away for life because if he did one crime he did them all. No one could fake the twenty cents on the eyes like he could. We knew that he was the one that started it all and we were going to finish it. Now it was time to focus on the next crime and it was time to get a look at who he was going to kill next.

It was going to be a poker player from Vegas staying with his girlfriend. They lived together but they were taking a break. There was always a chance he was going to kill someone different. He was always surprising us by killing these types of people. This was a different type of poker player because he had just won four million dollars in a televised event. This Vegas event had been something to watch because he had been down and out and he came back to win. He had quite the poker face and

I watched the whole thing. There was nothing bad about this guy. He was just visiting his girlfriend who was about to move with him and then he got killed the next day. This didn't change things for her because she didn't get any of the money. She didn't like big towns and she wasn't willing to move back from Vegas. It was something that they were trying to work out. It was a big commitment but in the end she won because she only loved him for his money. She was down on her luck and the cards were down on the table for everyone to see. There was no poker face and there was no one to say that it was going to be alright. There was nothing she could do but find another boyfriend. She was a beautiful young girl so finding another boyfriend wasn't totally out of the question. There was nothing that made sense about this killing.

He was shot in the head with a shotgun and usually it was a silenced pistol. It was different and this wasn't speaking to me saying that this was the serial killer. Maybe he was changing but this said copycat all the way. Maybe it was just the serial killer showing off how much balls he had and saying look at what I can do and still get away with it. He was showing off saying that he couldn't get caught. There was nothing that was going to get him caught unless he wanted to get into trouble with a gun felony or a small crime down the road. He was going to leave something behind when he wanted to get caught. I thought we would have some bloody clothes to compare to the shotgun we had found in the dumpster but we had no luck. We were 1 for 2 and I didn't like it. We were getting unlucky with no fingerprints. We had nothing and no one knew anything. I would believe in luck when a fairy cast her dust on the town. I was getting serious about investigating whatever I knew. I was looking over the crime scenes with a fine tooth comb. We went to all the stores and looked for purchases of shotguns and there was nothing so we gave up. We obviously had nothing so why were we trying? We got an address off the serial number of the gun. The person moved and we knew it wasn't the serial killer. That was a hit and miss but the neighbor told us that she could tell us what he looked like. We had a sketch artist draw a sketch and we put it on the air. It was going to get us somewhere. After a couple of years it was getting to the point where we had to mark the lead dead. He knew how to cover his tracks and he knew we were trying to find him. I knew the description was right but the killer was still killing and it was still frustrating. I was just going to keep looking at the crime scene photos and make myself go crazy trying to find him. There was nothing we were doing that was getting us anywhere.

Next he killed a gameshow host. He was on in the morning and he was doing his job like he did every morning. It was sad to say they had to replace him. People were going to be mad because they didn't like change. There was nobody like him. There was a lot of outrage and people wanted justice. I wanted justice when he was killing every day. I felt for these people because they were like family to me. He was killing every day and it wasn't fair. I wanted to kill someone that wasn't the serial killer. I wanted to kill myself for doing drugs and alcohol. I couldn't save myself from the drugs and the drinking. I wanted to stop but every time I stopped I would start again. There was gut rot that I had every day from the drinking. My teeth hurt from the drugs and I knew I was wearing away the enamel and my insides. The drugs were my only friend. I needed the drugs to forget all the heartache in my life.

The call that hurt me was my sister, my other niece and my nephews had died in a car crash. Dimes on their eyes, signature of the serial killer and he had cut the brakes. It was a different way to kill and I hated him for it. He said he would kill one of my family members and I hated him knowing he finally pulled it off. He was a monster and he was the monster in the closet that everyone was afraid of. There was nothing that I wanted to do but crawl in a hole and die. There was something that was changing about him. He had a different killing style and he was sick enough that he would resort to killing my family members. I was still getting into my drinking and drug habits. I was getting blacking out from drinking and going to work. I was a sad miserable mess wallowing in my own misery. There was always going to be that hurt of losing those family members. I was going to hunt him down and serve my own justice. Now it was going to me angry at the world. I was going to drink more now that I lost my sister. I was going to be more drugs that I because I lost my family members. They thought it was an accident that they got in a car accident but and I couldn't tell them otherwise. They didn't need to know that it was a serial killer. I asked the papers to leave it out. They did and the family read the paper and knew nothing. The family heard it from the news and knew that it was the serial killer. They blamed me again. I told the news to leave well enough alone but of course they didn't listen. I got my family to hate me again. It all seemed to bring my house of cards crumbling down.

The killing spree was continuing and it was another teenager. It was going to be another family without their child. There was a kid out there skateboarding and he was shot on the street. He was just an innocent kid going about his day and he had been shot. The serial killer drove off in a mustang convertible that was a 1967 model. There was no sense to shooting a sixteen year old kid. There was nothing the family could have done. He was skating around having fun with his friends. He was the victim of a random act of violence. The killer didn't care about anyone else but himself. He was just going around and having a good time. He was just going with his friends to the park. it was nothing a random act of violence. If it were my kid I wouldn't know what to do. Now he was dead in the street and I was investigating the crime. I was nothing more than a street cop investigating another crime. There was doubt in the division that we were ever going to solve these crimes. It was going to make me go nuts not knowing who was going to be killed next. The serial killer was too good to be caught. He had a special connection to me when he killed my family. I felt that everything happened for a reason. God did everything for a reason and that they were in a better place. Hopefully he didn't want to harm the rest of my family. If he did I wanted to catch him before it happened. There was something about him that was changing. He cut my sister's brakes in her car, he used a shotgun in a case where and he usually used a silenced pistol.

He also used an Uzi to gun down a teenager that was skateboarding. I didn't think this was making any sense. Why was he changing his means of killing? He was changing his killing style and it was weird to me. It was something I hadn't seen before. Usually serial killers were all about consistency. Sticking to the same routine and getting in the groove of what worked. A serial killer usually got caught in a week or sooner and but he was smarter than that. He was about consistency and leaving no clues behind and that was why he didn't get caught. The thing that worked for him was a silenced pistol so why change that? There was nothing that made sense on why he was changing his killing tactics now. He was just changing to toy with us. He would switch back and then go to a different killing style. It was something that we couldn't get a handle on.

He had stabbed someone in bed and that was just a sign of how far he was willing to go for a kill. There was something that made me sick to my stomach. There was a shotgun blast to the head. It was bloody and then the fact that it was to the head was something that made me throw up outside. There was blood all over the walls and blood on the bed made it even more of a mess. I had a weak stomach and it was something I wasn't aware of. I knew it was all the alcohol and drugs. I was hung over from the night before. I wasn't ready for the crime scene. I didn't have enough food in my stomach. There was a sad truth I had to deal with. It was the fact that I was a sad drunk with a drug problem. The cops didn't notice the alcohol on my breath. They realized I had a weak stomach with a lot of throw up at the crime scene. They didn't realize I had a drug problem. I realized I needed to check myself into AA and NA. There was nothing that was going to make this easy but I needed to do whatever it took to quit. I realized I didn't want to. I quit drugs for a while but I started showing up high to work. Then I stopped caring about work and stopped showing up. I wasn't serious about the NA or AA. There was nothing I wanted to do but get high and get drunk. It was a sad life and now it was obvious that I was showing up drunk and high to work. They talked to me and it was a talk I didn't care about. It was something I had to control if I was going to keep my job. I had to stop showing up to work high and drunk. I had to control my urges. I knew I could do it but it was going to be hard. I wanted to get high and drunk all the time but I knew I couldn't. I couldn't sleep or eat because I was getting drunk and high all the time. The drugs and drinking were affecting me all the time. It was affecting my sleep schedule. There was nothing that was making me sleep any better because of the meth. All of these drugs were keeping me up for days. The cocaine was numbing my body and it was numbing my sense of passion. The expenses were piling up and I didn't know what to do. The money wasn't good enough. I was spending all I was making and I couldn't figure it out. I needed more money and I was just going nuts on the drugs. There was nothing I could do but survive on the drugs and stay up for days. There was something about the drugs that made me feel so alive. It made me feel invincible like superman. I felt like it was my natural high but it was also my kryptonite. I was paying for every mistake I made and I knew the drugs would be my downfall. The expenses were getting ridiculous and I couldn't manage. I was at my breaking point and I needed to find a way to kick the drug habit. I quit drugs for a year and then started again. There was nothing I could do to quit for good. They would always be in my system and it would always be my weakness. I was having seizures and I needed to get out of this life. It was a curse that I needed to break out of. I was just getting away from what I believed in. I didn't need family even though they were reaching out to me. They were only reaching out to me because of my drug habit. They didn't want anything to do with my drug habit after I didn't listen. There was something that was bothering me. Why was this serial killer coming after my family? Did he want something from me? Did he want me to lose control and do something stupid? Did he want me off this case? I didn't know what he wanted from me and I didn't want to find out. I just wanted to find out who he was before he killed another one of my family members. I just want to kill him and make him suffer. There was going to be no chance of that. Someone was going to investigate the case and find him before I did. There was going to be justice done and he was going to be served on a silver platter. It was going to be sweet justice for me.

The next kill he made was a country singer that sang around local bars. She was known around neighboring cities. It was nice she had performed at our bar last night but she had been murdered the next morning. That was a tragedy that ended in a gruesome manner. She was in a hotel waiting to move onto the next bar and it was something that was going to be another one night performance. She got paid five hundred bucks every time she performed. It was a nice way to make a living and it was something that she loved to do. I was proud of her for making it so far on so much talent. I had seen her a couple of times when I had been drinking at the local bars. It was a good to watch when you were drinking. I had seen her at a couple of bars and slept with her a couple of times. She was very attractive and it was something that was good enough to get attention in the news. It wasn't like any of the other kills because every kill was unique. There was a lot of press about this kill. The kill was in the papers and this was nothing compared to what it was going to be in the next couple of days. It was taking people by surprise that the cops hadn't caught this serial killer after five years. He was the hardest serial killer to catch in my ten years of being a cop. There was nothing harder than being a cop and not being able to catch serial killer. There was nothing I could say that was going to make this any easier for the family. We had dated for a couple of months after we had slept together. They were some of the happiest months and I was happy with her. There was something about her that I liked. There was something about her that drew me in. She was like a magnet where people were attracted to her personality. Her personality was bubbly and she was an outgoing person and loved talking with new people. She loved going on dates but she wasn't going to be the one to sleep with you until she knew you were the one. she liked to dance out at nightclubs and have fun. She knew how to have fun when we were dating. When I was with her I had a lot of fun. When I was with her it was like there was no one else in the world. There was no one I was dating now because I was doing drugs and alcohol. I didn't want anyone to see that side of me. I had a rage problem when I did drugs and alcohol. There was that side of me that no one else knew but my family. It was that side of me that came out at the wrong times. It got me in trouble and I knew if I was going to quit it had to be the right time. There was nothing that I wanted to do but get drunk and high. I didn't want to go into work anymore. There was nothing I wanted to do besides a slob. I wanted to get my life back together again but I didn't know how. Without the alcohol and drugs I didn't know how to function. The alcohol and drugs were affecting my life in a way I didn't know how to explain. It was taking over and I didn't want to go to work. I wasn't sure how to catch this serial killer. There was nothing we could catch him on. There was nothing that was going to put him behind bars. There was a lot of work we had to do to catch him. We had a lot of things we were trying to do to find him. We were looking at all the crime scene photos. We were also trying to find witnesses but there were none. We had nothing and we knew it. We were at a dead end and we had to turn around. We realized that the serial killer had the drop on us. He was going to kill again until we could catch him or until he wanted to stop. We knew we had to do something. We were like a dog chasing a car. We were chasing it knowing we would never catch it.

Now he was breaking into houses killing people. It was stupid that we couldn't get him on footprints from glass. There was nothing that we could get from it. He would sweep up the glass and throw it in the garbage can and put it in his car and drive it to a landfill. He knew that if he put it in the landfill there would be no evidence to trace him to the crime. He was smarter than us. It was getting tiring trying to catch him. it was going to be a pain in the ass trying to catch him. It was going to be a mindset of were we going to catch him? There was doubt that we were going to catch him among all the cops. There was nothing that we were doing right. We couldn't fit all the pieces of the puzzle together, what made him tick, how could we get inside his head, how could we catch this guy? Now it was a test of how we could figure out what type of person he was going to kill next so we could prepare for it.

He killed a curler coming home from Canada to visit his parents. It was something that we weren't prepared for. He was training and it was just that he all year when he wasn't doing it for real. He did this in his free time but he liked fishing and he played hockey. He really didn't do much else besides work at a bar for a profession. He was killed seeing his parents. His parents weren't killed and that was what I found to be odd. The serial killer was in and out without a peep. He was the lucky one to die or unlucky as luck would have it. There was a target that he had. The bartender was the target and that was just what was on order. There was nothing that would keep the serial killer from killing him. I thought that it was weird because it was a stabbing. It was silent with his mouth duct taped and covered. A knife to the throat. There was a sense of urgency when he got stabbed numerous times on the body. They were all quick shallow stabs and it was like he wanted to get it over with. It wasn't a crime of passion. It was just weird he had chosen to stab again. It took us all by surprise and I was just shocked that the parents didn't hear a thing. Now it was something that was going to get in the paper for all the town to read about. There was ninety thousand people in this town so he was going to have to kill a lot of people. If he wanted to make a dent in the population he was going to have to kill a lot of people. If he made a dent in the population it was going to make the headlines. It made me sick how many people he had killed. He was killing and we weren't doing anything about it. We hadn't caught him in seven years and it was frustrating. There was going to be a lot of people that were going to be mad at us. We didn't catch any major serial killers and we made the point of relying on evidence. He had killed for so long and we had showed no progress in catching him. There was no evidence to put him away so what could we do? He was on a major killing spree and it was just going to grow every day. It was going to be a lot of press. It was going to grab the attention of every person in this town making people wonder what the cops were doing to stop him. There was nothing to do if we had no evidence. There was going to be a price to pay if he didn't get caught. We had to find the evidence to put him away and we had to put the pieces together to build a strong case. There was no doubt he had to go down for all these crimes. These crimes were heinous and some of them were brutal. Some of them were hard to handle, especially for the police. There was nothing the police could do to stop this serial killer. There was nothing that the serial killer was doing that was a mistake. He could kill as much as he wanted without the cops being able to catch him.

The next kill he made was an electrician and he made it look like an accident. He crossed wires and put the wires to his chest and left it there for a couple of minutes until he died and that was the end of it. It was just a cruel death. It was a sick and cruel way to die. There was a painful side to that death. It took about three minutes for that death to occur and I wouldn't want to die that way. The only reason we determined it was a murder was the fact that he left the two dimes on the eyelids. There was the evidence we needed in court to convict him if it ever went to court. There was a method to this madness and it made us all crazy. That was a saying of mine and it worked in my favor. I was dealing with that myself when I was drinking. There was nothing that was making me go insane besides my drinking, drugs and this serial killer. I was debating retirement but retirement wasn't in the cards until I caught this serial killer. With this serial killer behind bars I could finally rest easier at night. With him killing my time card could be punched at any moment. I could be next at any moment so I had to have my head on a swivel for myself and my family. There was nothing I wouldn't do for my family and my family deserted me a long time ago. They deserted me when my brother, sister, nieces and nephews died. It was a tragedy but it was all in the past. Now it was time to leave it all behind and catch this bastard and kill him the only way I knew how, with a fight he wouldn't forget. He believed I was supposed to be a cop first. I was the law for a long time and I was going to kill him whether it was self- defense or not. I was going to get my fair share of criticism from my cop buddies for drinking and drugs. They knew I was going to the strip clubs after hours but it didn't matter because it was all a misfortune that I had. I was boozing and doing drugs all the time so I had my own personal issues to deal with and I was in my own hell. Hell is what you make it and I made it my life. Life isn't worth living if you're in your own personal hell all the time. There was no time for anything else besides drinking and doing drugs at home. Usually before the drinking drugs I would watch Netflix. I would have watched forensic files and numbers. Now all I was known for was sleeping with hookers and staying home to watch Netflix. It was something that I did on a regular basis and I didn't care. I was reluctant to get a good girl but I was not going to find a wife anytime soon. I was looking in all the wrong places like the bars. I was now drinking at bars and doing drugs at home and it was pathetic. I was just a washed up cop who couldn't catch a serial killer that was smarter than him. There was no way that I was going to catch this serial killer without clues. He was smarter than me and the whole squad and we knew it. We were just chasing our tails and chasing a ghost. We were against a guy that had killed three thousand people and he wasn't even done. The body count was going up and I couldn't tell you how many people he was killing every day. He was just killing people that didn't deserve to die.

He killed a clown at the carnival and that was his latest kill. He killed him with a sniper rifle on a ride. No one got a look at him. He blended in and he killed the guy that operated the ride because he was the only witness. He blended in with the crowd and he got away. People were scared of him. He was intimidating in nature and I knew if I ever met him it would be death. They feared that they would be next. Now we were on the hunt for someone that no one could identify. We lost him in the crowd. There were a lot of people that were scared of him. There were a lot of people thinking that the hourglass of time was running out. They were locking their windows and doors at night but it wasn't helping. He was still breaking in and we knew desperate times called for desperate measures. He was killing numerous people and he was on the hunt for prey. He was killing anyone he could get his hands on. It was awful because the people were in fear. He was killing because he had no other hobbies. He wasn't raping these woman which meant there was no DNA. It made us wonder why he was abducting so many women. Maybe he just liked tying up women to torture them to have some fun. Maybe he was just twisted in a way we had never seen before. There was nothing that was left at the house as far as clues. There was nothing from the house that was stolen. He didn't want money or jewelry which meant he must have a good job. He had a day job because he was killing at night. It lead nowhere which meant it might have been a bad memory. There was nothing to be done. We had no leads and we had no one to tell us anything. We had no hope in the lion's den. There was nothing to do but hope and pray. There was always a chance that he could screw up but this far in it was unlikely. There was nothing more frustrating than having nothing and knowing nothing. He was killing all our witnesses and every time we got something it didn't pan out. How can all those people in the carnival see the serial killer and not come up with a positive sketch? It makes no sense to me. There is no room for guessing because a guess is just a theory that leads nowhere. The facial features weren't good enough and we were back to the drawing board. There was no way we could solve this without the sketch. That was our only lead. We had the cops at the carnival but they said they didn't get a good look at him. That was a bust and now we were at square one again. That was our luck all through this case. We knew we had to change the way we looked at this case and our methods. Now it was time to go back to the drawing board. We asked the witnesses what the serial killer was driving. They said he was driving a red Kia. There were three thousand red Kia cars in the city so that didn't help. We weren't going to narrow that down because we didn't have time. Now that he was breaking into houses no one was safe. Everyone was fearing for their lives. There was nothing that people could do to protect themselves. I needed to catch this serial killer if it was the last thing I did. He was getting on all our nerves. There was a growing pain and he was the root of all of it. He was causing my drinking and drug problem. The drugs were like bugs under the skin. It was like an itch that wouldn't go away. Sure it was my fault that I was doing drugs and alcohol but I was doing it because I couldn't solve these cases. These cases were taking a toll on all of us. These cases were making us all go to our vices. There was a nagging suspicion that this serial killer was related to the last twenty cent killer. I was growing tired of playing the serial killer's games of cat and mouse. Why was I always the cat that could never catch the mouse? I couldn't even find the mouse. The mouse kept hiding in its little hole in the wall. It was pissing me off and I didn't know what I could do about it. There was nothing I could do about it because he was too good. I was going to catch him at some point but the question was when. When were we going to catch him and how many people was he going to kill before we caught him? That was the question on everybody's mind. There was nothing the public wanted more than to sleep at night. I wanted this guy dead by my hand. I wanted it to be like the old west. Shoot first ask questions later.

The next kill he made was a priest and he was stabbed thirty seven times. It was something of a massacre. It was at a church and I figured you couldn't get more ironic than that. It was on a Sunday after hours and it was smart enough to make me blush. The priest only stayed behind for five minutes and I figured he was in a hurry to leave. There was nothing about it that was civilized. The killer wanted to be fast but he took his time and got out before the cops arrived. He cleaned up the blood with a mop and the mop had blood without fingerprints. The blood of the priest was all we found and it was very clean. No one saw the serial killer and we knew they were just scared. It was a quick getaway with screeching tires and muddy footprints. He had stabbed before so this was nothing different. He was used to stabbing people and taking out his rage. There were a lot of times that he had stabbed his victims so we knew he was getting comfortable. It was almost as common for him as shooting someone in the head. Stabbings were becoming his go to kill. There was nothing that was different about this. It was like a routine and we needed to break his habit. He was killing a lot more elderly people and this was also routine for him. He would always kill one random person. He wouldn't kill the same person with the same job twice. That was something we had noticed. It was a pattern that he never broke and that was great because we always knew it was something we could count on. Just like him we had the routine of eating at the same coffee and donut place once a week. That was why we were getting so fat. It was becoming a habit for him because they were weak easy targets. They usually forgot to set their alarms or they were hard of hearing. There was nothing that was sad about these killings. Once you started feeling emotions for these victims was the point where you started to lose your mind. You also started questioning whether you wanted to be a cop or not. This was testing my emotions whether I wanted to do drugs and whether I wanted to have a relationship. I was really questioning whether I wanted to be a cop. Did I want to be a cop or did I want to retire and let someone else catch this serial killer? Then I realized I had to see this one through. If I quit now I would never know who this serial killer was. I needed to know if this serial killer needed the silencer for his gun. I was nothing more than a cop that couldn't catch a serial killer. There was nothing that I could do to raise my self-esteem and catch this serial killer. We had a lead that he drove a red Kia but it wasn't stolen. If it wasn't stolen then it must have been his vehicle. We had a lot of leads on how many vehicles he drove. It was so crazy to think he drove all these vehicles. There was nothing we could do and if we were doing it then it wasn't working.

There was a car crash and it was determined that the brakes were cut. It was the serial killer and he was making a habit of changing his killing style. He had cut someone's brakes to make it so they would get in a crash without anyone noticing. There is nothing that is scarier than knowing you are going to die. There is nothing worse than waiting to die because then you don't want to drive into work. You don't want to go to work knowing you could be next every second of every day. It seems like every day simple tasks make you scared.

There was a murder up the street from where I lived. There were blood and guts splattered all over the street and I realized that could be me one day. It was a crime scene that would make you lose your lunch if you had a weak stomach. There was a cop there that threw up at the crime scene and there was no evidence. It was one bullet to the back of the head with messy results. How could such a messy crime scene have no evidence? There was a bullet to the back of the head and it was a taxi driver. It was a well-dressed taxi driver that recognized the boss. He obviously wasn't from around here to dress like that. There was something that was out of the ordinary at the crime scene. He had no wallet and his stomach was cut open. There was rage and that was out of the ordinary. There was theory thrown out that the serial killer had taken the cab. There were a lot of theories about this case but they were only theories. We only had theories and we needed more ideas. This was going to be a tough case like all the others. There was nothing that I could do to solve this case. It was hard to look into this case and find any clues. There were a few donuts left on my desk and I ate them to try and get ideas. I looked at the foot impressions and the skid marks of the car. They were the 1972 dodge charger. There were only 76 made in this town. There were latex gloves with no fingerprints in them. I ate another donut and got another idea. There were no fingerprints on the outside but the inside would have fingerprints. I checked and they weren't in the system. This was starting to annoy me. Our first solid lead and it went nowhere. Maybe we could check the sweat and compare that to the fingerprints. There was nothing I could do but hope for the best and get a clue in the next case.

The next case was a blown up orphanage. There was nothing left of the orphanage but dust and ashes. All the kids were charred and their teeth were blown out of their mouth. There were adults in there too but most of them were kids. The bombs were placed in the orphanage the night before. It was a tragedy that won't be forgotten. There were so many dead kids. Only a monster would do this.

There was a bomb set off in the fire station and eight firefighters died. It took two years to rebuild with raised funds from the community. There was nothing to do but mourn their deaths. There was a lot of death destruction lately and most of the cops didn't know what to make of it. There was nothing that was going to make this any better. We needed to come together as a community and make people realize that they weren't alone. We didn't know how he knew to make bombs. It made me sick to think you could kill kids and live with yourself. There was no sense to killing little children. Killing children was a new kind of low. There was a certain kind of hell for people like him and I knew I was going to see him rot in hell for this. I was going to make sure that people in jail knew that he killed children in an orphanage. There was nothing that was going to save him in prison and I was going to make sure he died in prison. He was going to make people unhappy with killing all these people. It made me want to rip off his skin. Someone was going to turn him in. I was going to get him and make him pull his gun and then I was going to kill him. That was how he was going to die. There was going to be a day where he was going to stop killing. When that day came people would be able to sleep better at night. There was nothing that made me sleep well at night knowing he was still killing. There was nothing that would suggest he was going to come into my house. Just in case he did I was going to shoot and kill him. I was prepared for anyone that came into my house. They were going to die if they broke into my house.

There was another dead cop on the streets. He had put a lot of drug dealers away while he was on the force. He had rescued a few people from burning houses and it was a true act of heroism. It was something his family could be proud of. Putting drug dealers away saved a lot of teenagers from drugs and overdoses. Now he was dead and his wife wouldn't see him return home. She had reported him missing after he didn't come home last night. He turned up dead the next morning. There was nothing that was more tragic than a dead cop. There was nothing that could have been done to save him. He was another dead and gone cop that would be missed. There was going to be a lot of people at his funeral. There was going to be a lot of blood on the serial killer's hands. All the cops were going to be after him and there was going to be riots. There was nothing that was going to happen to him that was going to be written in the papers even if they tortured him.

The next kill was a little girl that was in commercials. This girl had been in three commercials in two months. It was pretty good money for her. Her name was plastered all over the T.V in those couple of months. She was in a Sprite commercial and another commercial I didn't watch. There was nothing I felt for this girl. I felt no emotion because if I felt sadness for people I couldn't do my job anymore. It would get in the way of my job. There was nothing that I felt for anybody when they died. I couldn't feel sadness for my family because it would show weakness at the lowest point of my life. Maybe if my cousin died I might be sad but other than that I wouldn't care. There was nothing I cared about anymore. There were a lot of people dying and I didn't know if I could handle it. There were all these people being killed and it was out of control. I didn't want it to continue. There was no one in the office that was understanding how he was getting away. There was nothing that I wanted to do more than kill this serial killer. I also didn't want to kill him and go to jail. I had to be smart and think like him. There was something I had to do and that was get this serial killer and put him behind bars. There was nothing but good cops working on this case. That wasn't enough for me because I needed forensics and more results. There was no forensics, no evidence and we needed both to convict him. There was nothing we could do but wait case after case and get nowhere. Everyone was losing their minds getting frustrated. They were going to long lengths to try and catch this serial killer with no results. We were getting no results. We were getting nowhere and it was frustrating. We had no idea who he was and everybody was wondering what his job was. The cocaine was coursing through my veins and the booze was taking over my life. The booze was a compulsion of mine. The cocaine and meth kept me up for days. Those drugs kept me sharp enough to look over those case files. There was nothing to find. The serial killer was too good at his job. He wasn't going to leave anything behind at the crime scenes. He was beating us at our own game and we knew we had to play our game. I wasn't the good cop I once was. Good cops caught serial killers and I wondered when that time was going to come. That was the gift of a good cop. Catching a serial killer took skill and dedication and those were things that I didn't have. There was nothing I could do to catch him. I was getting frustrated and I was never going to catch him. I didn't want to give up even though the odds seemed to be stacked against me. I had to keep pursuing him and not lose my cool. I needed to catch him and then retire for good. There was a retiring factor after I was done. With this serial killer it made people go crazy. There was nothing that was going to bring me out of retirement. I was going into retirement and I was going to take many vacations. If I could I would have already retired. I was going to go fishing more often and get my tan. I was going to get fat on a beach somewhere. I was going to love my wife and have some more kids. There was going to be a good retirement. Nothing seemed better than my wife and kids. I had a lazy cat that liked to sleep eat. He looked out the window longing to roam free from the world of the indoors. That would be the life, just having the life of a cat. The only thing to worry about is worrying about your next meal and when your next nap is going to take place. There was nothing easier than being a cat and being lazy. I was being a cop for too long and the serial killer was killing for too long. His killing spree was lasting too long. It was lasting for seven years so far and it was racking up six thousand kills. There was no way we could stop him. There was too much killing. It was a massacre that was going to stand the tests of time. There was all this blood and change in killing style. I knew there was nothing I could do to stop it. There was no way we could keep up with all the crime scenes. We had so many cops looking on in the night wondering what we could do. Now it was turning into a serious killing spree. It was all coming down like a house of cards. It was all too much killing for us. We couldn't keep up with this killing. We put out a manhunt for him with no results. He was nowhere to be found. He was just too good to be found. There was all this killing in one night. We had all these cops helping and too much money invested. There were no results and it was just a jurisdiction issue. We weren't going to give up these cases. We had invested too much and they agreed. There was nothing worse than a jurisdiction issue. They took our crime scene photos and we were forced to work with them. We figured out that we didn't work well with others. They figured out this wasn't their type of work and gave us everything they had. It wasn't much but it generated a lead. I was baffled that we weren't able to catch this serial killer after seven years and six thousand bodies. All these traumatized families that had to go through loss and heart wrenching pain. They knew we were doing nothing besides sitting on our hands waiting for the next kill.

There was a karate instructor that turned up dead the next day. We were suspicious suspecting he could protect himself and throw a few blows. It was over in a few minutes and it appeared he had in fact broken an arm and we called a few hospitals. They said they couldn't release that kind of information. Not only were there twenty stab wounds on the victim we suspected that the serial killer cut himself. It was just tragic because now the family members were going to have to find a different karate instructor to go to. There was going to be a lot of angry parents. The kids weren't going to have an after school activity. Now it was time to find a different karate instructor. It was the perfect opportunity to do drugs since my work schedule was changing. I needed to do drugs at a different time. I was still high from the day before hoping it didn't affect my work. There was nothing worse than drugs affecting my work. My work was the only good thing I had left. My drugs and alcohol were the only things I had to look forward to. There was something about this serial killer that was peculiar. It was like he was in the criminal justice field or trained in the criminal justice field. He was very smart like he read criminal justice books. There was that quality about him that I found very smart. There was something about him that bothered me. There was a certain quality about him that said punch me in the face. I was going on a theory that the serial killer was a girl. I was going to take that theory to the grave. It was only time that was going to tell. That was going to be it for me and I was going to watch a few movies to calm my nerves. I wanted to drink some coffee but it wasn't going to go with the drugs I was taking. The coffee wasn't going to mix with cocaine. I haven't eaten in three days and it was something that was pathetic. I felt weak and I was staying up for weeks on end. There was a feeling of emptiness when I took cocaine. The next three days I would be starving and take marijuana. It was a vicious circle of drugs that was never going to stop. There was that factor of going through phases and never giving up on myself. There was nothing I liked about myself anymore because I was a junkie. I was a booze hound that couldn't function without his vices. There was a side to me that no one knew. I didn't like what I had become. I wanted to change but I didn't know how. The first step was admitting that I needed to change. I was different than everyone on the force because they were all sober. With all the drugs and booze I had been doing I expected to be dead by now. The fact that I wasn't was a surprise. There was nothing I wanted more than to die after I caught this serial killer because I had nothing else to live for. There was a lot of family of mine left and I didn't care for a single one of them. They were all against me and I didn't care. The job came first and the booze and drugs came second. There was something that was troubling me, how could the serial killer go seven years without getting caught? There was no sense to this madness. The madness was continuing and I could hardly handle it. There was madness in the streets and we were lucky we weren't trying to catch any other serial killers. There was nothing worse than trying to catch multiple serial killers. There was always going to be serial killers but none as good as this serial killer. There was nothing that was going to be sweeter than catching this serial killer.

The next kill was a college baseball pitcher and it was a pitcher with a 2.72 ERA and it was pretty good. It made for a pretty good baseball pitcher and I was pretty impressed. There was a good player in all of us and I was just going crazy. It was all good people that he was killing. It was model citizens that he was killing. He was killing recently released criminals and it was a tragedy. The family was furious that it had to be their kid and it was the end of the chapter in the book of his life. My life was a good life minus the drinking and drugs and my family not talking to me.

My brother sister nieces and nephews were dead but my other sister was alive. It was just like she was dead because she didn't want to talk to me either. It was like they were all dead because they were all dead to me. They were going to be in my life when they died and that was it for me. I was going to be at their funerals when they died and that was going to be it.

There was a case I was on where a family member's friend was murdered. I figured it out and it was a serial killer and it was the first time I had solved a case for a friend of mine. There was nothing I could have done to save that friend's family member. It was a tragedy that she had to die. I was there to console my friend because it was a hard time for both of us. There was grieving, a large turnout for a funeral and a lot of food and gathering for a get together after the funeral. There was a lot of mourning about a week after the funeral and the whole school remembered him. The football team played in his honor and that was very nice of them.

They were all great that way and there were a lot of great kids that cared for him and he had a lot of good friends at school. Now it was time to focus on the future of my career on catching this serial killer and then retiring in the Bahamas. There was a lot of beaches there and I could tan there and get a lot of drinks there and enjoy my retirement.

I was thinking about it and now there was a hooker dead in the streets. It was a pretty girl and her parents were outside the yellow police tape. They were crying like they should be and they didn't know she was into this type of career. They wouldn't know since they hadn't talked to her in quite some time. There were a lot of things they didn't know. The pimp that was controlling her was also her boyfriend. There was also the fact that the pimp that was controlling her was beating her up on a regular basis. It was a sad truth that the parents didn't know about but it was a cold world out there. It was something that the parents didn't need to know and they didn't need to be involved with this case. They didn't need to know what we knew. There was nothing that we knew and we were going to know nothing for a while. I was getting sick of going to crime scenes and learning nothing. It was getting sickening getting no clues and no evidence. There was nothing I was getting out of this crime scene. It was just getting to me and I needed to know what I was getting myself into. I was getting into something that I couldn't get myself out of. I was out of my league thinking I could catch this serial killer. He was so much better than me. I had the attitude that I was never going to catch him unless he wanted to be caught. There was something bothering me, he told me that I would catch him when he got bored of killing. How could you just get bored of killing altogether? It made no sense to me but what did I know? It was going to be a hard case to solve but I was like a drug sniffing dog. I was going to sniff out the drugs and find them even though they were hidden. There was something that bothered me, this killer was very meticulous like he was in the law enforcement profession or read up on law books or something like that. It was something that gave him the edge over us and he was better than us. He was better than us in every way and he was going to outsmart us until we caught him in the end. There was something that was going to catch him in the end. There was going to be a fingerprint or he was going to get cocky. He was going to get greedy and get messy. He was going to forget that we were chasing him. There was going to be something that he missed at a crime scene that was going to get him caught. There was nothing that was going to get him caught anytime soon but in the distant future I was going to catch him.

The next kill was a scientist. He had sulfuric burns all over his face. It was in the scientist's lab and he was a good scientist that was highly respected. That was convenient for the serial killer because he got it from the lab as the scientist was leaving the lab. He dumped it on the scientists face when he was in the lab and it was a quick death. There was nothing that was civilized about this killing. It was pretty gruesome in my mind. His face was disfigured and I didn't like the crime scene. The floor was melted all the way through and we could see through to the next level. It was a murder that was ironic because it was an acid that was found in the lab. I didn't know what sulfuric acid was used for but I knew it should be locked up. It was kill that was he had never committed before. He was changing his killing style for now and we didn't know why. He was going to kill a different person with a different type of job at some point. Everything had a tipping point and our tipping point was this case. We knew he was changing and we didn't know why. He was killing out of his comfort zone. We didn't know what drove him to this kill because he could have spilled it on himself. There was nothing that was making him mad that we knew of. There was nothing that was setting him off and to us that was scary. A killer with no switch was dangerous because we didn't know what set him off. I think he was killing because he could get away with it. He was going to kill until we would link him to something in his past. There was a method to his madness, kill as many people as you can before you get caught. There was nothing that made sense about this case, why kill this scientist with sulfuric acid? It didn't make any sense to me. It was so brutal to me to disfigure a person like that. There was no sense to it and it made me sick. He was killing because he wanted to taunt us. There was nothing that made sense anymore. This was nothing more than a criminal getting off from killing and taunting police. Police are working hard to catch a serial killer and having no results. Now we are having a sulfuric acid incident with a scientist? How cruel. There was something that was changing with this serial killer and that was his killing style. He becomes more brutal of a human being every day. By killing and taunting us and not leaving behind fingerprints or clues that meant we were dealing with a professional. That was his theme and it was working. I wanted to meet this serial killer and get inside his head. I wanted to pick his brain and get a view of what he was like. He was someone that killed for sport and fun. That was a dual combination that was dangerous. I didn't want to live in a world like that. There was nothing that made him tick because he just killed people for fun. His cockiness was going to be his downfall. At some point of his killing spree was going to come to an end and I was going to be the one to end it. You can mark my words that I was going to catch and kill him. Now it was time to investigate another crime.

The crime was a physicist that died from sulfuric acid over the face. It was gruesome and we knew it was exactly like the last crime. There was nothing that was different in this kill, it was the exact same in every way. I was getting tired of people dying. It was a hassle being at these crime scenes. It was all the same. Go to the crime scene, investigate the murder, and find no clues. I was sick of having no clues at these crime scenes, and getting mad all the time. I was feeling like the cops at the office were giving up. I was starting to give up too. There was no hope of going on after all these cases. There was nothing in the evidence locker because there was no evidence. All of these crimes had no evidence and I was tired of investigating these crimes and having no evidence. The evidence wasn't there and there was nothing to investigate. I was frustrated along with every other cop investigating the serial killer. What we were after wasn't fool's gold. We also weren't about to hand it off to someone else. We were going to be the ones investigating everything. We were getting overwhelmed and getting the clues that no one else knew about.

I got a girlfriend when all seemed lost. She was a girl studying forensics and investigating a serial killer. She was very good at her job and for me it was just good to be dating again. I quit drugs and alcohol. I was clean the whole time I was with her and I felt safe again. I was with her and there was nothing that was more important. I was eating my meal and she was having a casual drink and I realized she liked her drinks. She was just a casual drinker. She drank a lot when she was with friends at bars like we all do. It was what we all did and that was what my sister used to do. My other sister didn't touch a drop of alcohol. That was something that you did either because you didn't like it or because you didn't find any reason to drink. There was a problem with this serial killer, he kept changing his means of killing. Now was the time to catch him in the act but it wasn't going to happen. We needed to decide what our motives were for catching this serial killer were. There was nothing I hated worse than trying to catch this twenty cents killer. I couldn't catch a serial killer that was so elusive after such a long period of time. There was a time where I was putting serial killers away like night and day. I was the best at it and we were putting away serial killers left and right. Our police department was the best at putting away serial killers. When we put away rapists we would celebrate with a drink. It was a great time and it doesn't happen anymore. There was a time where we were the best at putting away criminals. Now I was feeling like one of the worst cops in the world. I was feeling like I wasn't accomplishing anything. I was feeling like a failure. I was feeling like I was doing nothing to catch this serial killer. I was going to retire after all of this. I had to retire on a good note. There were no good notes and I needed something to believe in. It couldn't be worse than it was now with all the low points that I had now. I was just hitting rock bottom by this point. I felt like the lowest piece of scum right now. There was nothing to lift my spirits besides my kids. I was wrong because I was going to be over the hill before the serial killer was caught. I was going to pushing fifty which I considered old. I was going to be going to be pissed off by the time I caught him. I promised myself that I would catch him in a couple of years before retirement age. I don't break promises to myself or anyone else. I was going to go to work every day pressing on and doing my job. I work the same cases looking at evidence and pictures of victims. It helps me remember where I come from and what makes me human. I looked to see if there was anything I had missed. There was a kid in the nineties that had set church fires and that was up the victim's alley. I knew if I looked at this case long enough it would ring a bell. I had to look at this case closely and ask some questions. People would remember this because it was history and a teenager knew to leave behind evidence. The truth was we had to look in places no one wanted to look. The drug sniffing dog that was coming out in me. Maybe I would get lucky this time and break the case wide open. I was flying off the handle at my co- workers and I didn't mean to. They were just a product of me not catching the serial killer and they were in the crossfire. The crossfire had hit them like a stray bullet. It was like I was the stray bullet and they were the targets. I was going crazy not catching this serial killer. It was affecting my health not slowing down on my drinking and doing all these drugs. There was a mistake on my part by not looking at the footprints more closely. There was a footprint at the crime scene that I didn't think was useable but it was. It was useable but without a suspect it was useless. We knew he lived in the radius of these killings. He killed in his comfort zone which was in a few miles of his house. There was no way to determine this without knowing who he was. I was going to find out who he was. The whole squad that was working on this trying to figure out who he was. Now he was killing all sorts of people. It didn't narrow down what he did for a job or how much he made for a living. That wasn't helping us and that would have been a big clue for us. I was hoping we would find out who he was soon so we could save the next victim. The next victim wasn't going to be saved and it was going to be a tragedy. I was not going to have any feelings for the family that lost someone. If I did that I would be questioning my life as a policeman. This serial killer was very smart. He was smarter than all of us. We knew we had to catch him on our terms and that meant we might have to fight dirty. I knew how to fight dirty because I played bad cop in interrogation all the time. I liked playing bad cop but I was better at playing good cop. I knew how to make the bad guy my friend and make him confess. Making him confess was my specialty. I gave him the option of confessing or spending his time in prison. When he called his lawyer he usually told him to deal because he was in deep shit. It was all in my favor by that time and they knew it. I was a good cop back then and look at me now. I couldn't catch a serial killer. It was pathetic and it was a career that was sad to look at and I knew I had to do something fast. I needed to prove something to myself. It made us all look like bad cops. It made the captain look like he was never going to give us any time off. No vacations for any of us and we were in it for the long haul. I was going to make it out of here looking like I was the worst cop to lead the division. It looked bad for all of us. I was demoted and I was like all the other cops so where I wasn't in charge of anything. It was all bull crap and I didn't care anymore. I was getting paid less than I was before and I didn't like it. After a while I was drinking more and I couldn't afford it. I was just getting more depressed. It was taking a toll on me because I was coughing up blood. I was throwing up a lot more and eating less. I was smoking pot to try and eat. I was doing cocaine and not sleeping for days. I was staying awake and thinking about all the ways I could catch the serial killer. There were no ideas to catch the serial killer and I knew we needed something. This serial killer was doing anything he wanted whenever he wanted. There was nothing any of us could do to catch him. I was just a drunk washed up cop with his best years behind him. I was hoping to catch him on a silly whim. I was hoping I pulled the trigger to kill him. He deserved it for killing all those people. He could get the death penalty but that takes five or ten years. A bullet would suffice and I would pull the trigger if it came down to it. I was going to stop thinking about it before I drove myself crazy. Now I was going to have a drink and quit for good. Then that turned into ten and then it turned into a fourth of a bottle of Jack Daniels. That turned into blacking out. I was a sad miserable drunk and I didn't like myself. I couldn't drink Jack straight so I drank it with doctor pepper. There was a lot of alcohol at my house and I was going to drink it all. God was watching over me and making sure I didn't die of alcohol poisoning. There was nothing I did better than drinking and drugs. There was nothing better than drugs, alcohol and sex. There was something that said it could come to an end.

I got a call that my mother had died in a hit and run. Two dimes on her eyelids meant it was the serial killer. I knew he was trying to ruin my family relationship and I didn't care. It was already ruined and it was something that was weird. I was a disgrace to the family and they knew it. I was depressed and that's why I drank. I needed time to adjust to him killing all these people in one week. I was never home and I needed someone to love. There was no one for me to love. That was taking a toll on me as well. My wife had left me and taken the kids. I was sleeping with hookers and I didn't care about diseases. I was sleeping around with married woman. It was nice not to be tied down. I had girlfriends here and there but there was nothing serious. Then I got hung over and slept with someone that I shouldn't have. We were in love and we were just head over heels for each other. We were perfect for each other and we had so much in common. Then one day I came home and she was murdered and I knew it was him. I was pissed and I knew there was nothing I could do about it. I was upset and I didn't want anyone else. and there was a note to read.

"I've been watching you working alone and drinking yourself to death. How do you expect anyone to love you after all of that?

I want you all to myself

Sincerely the twenty cents killer."

He was a sick man and I couldn't handle the truth. I was just heartbroken that someone I loved died. She had wanted me to quit drinking and stop drugs but I wasn't ready. That was one of her conditions to staying with me. I stopped and then she was murdered. Now I could get back to drinking and drugs. Now it was back to the regular lifestyle again. My lifestyle was going to be in jeopardy if I found another a girlfriend. I was not going to have another girlfriend to ruin that lifestyle. I was going to find a girlfriend when I was ready to quit my lifestyle. If I was ready to quit then I would but until then it would never happen. When I was going to least expect it that was when I was going to catch the serial killer. I was running away from my problems. My problems were committing to a relationship and loving someone besides myself. I was so committed to drugs and alcohol. Those were the only things that I wanted to do. That was the only thing I was good at. There was nothing that the serial killer could take away from me that he hadn't already taken away. It was sickening to think that he could wipe out the rest of my family with one more blow. There was one more person he could kill and that was me. That would be a plus because I was already dead inside. I was impressed by how many people he had killed but that didn't mean I wasn't sorry for all the families that had lost someone. I was lost for words for the families that had lost someone. I didn't know what to tell them when they called. They were always asking what we were doing to catch this serial killer and we had no answer. There was nothing that we could tell them because there were no suspects, no witnesses, and no evidence. There was nothing we had so what could we tell them? It was a sad story for all of them but if we didn't have anything we weren't going to tell them anything. When they complained we weren't doing anything we told them we were working as hard as we could. We had nothing so that was what we were going to tell them. If we had nothing that was what we were going to work with. You worked with what the serial killer gave you and in this case it was nothing. I was frustrated but I couldn't let it show like so many times before.

My cop associates knew my anger and alcohol problems. Maybe they were related and as much as I didn't want that to be true they suspected it all the same. They knew my heavy drug problems and they knew I couldn't control it. When they asked me to stop I said I had it under control and gave them the how dare you ask me to stop act. I knew I couldn't control these problems. I was killing myself with these problems and I was going to make myself go crazy drinking and doing drugs. I was going to die an early death and not have no one at my funeral. They didn't care about me and I didn't care about me either. I was sad for them that they alienated me but then again they were jerks for alienating me. They thought they could place every family death on me but that wasn't how it worked. There was nothing about those deaths that was my fault. In their heart's they knew it but they didn't want to admit it. They wanted to pass the blame onto me. They wanted to pass the blame onto me to get over the grief. The pain of losing a loved one doesn't mean you should cut me out of your life. I was alienated for the fact that he died for both of us. I was investigating the same case. They thought I should have protected my big brother better. Maybe I could have been there for him when he died. Maybe I was the bad guy for losing my cool at the crime scene and never loving him like I should have. There was nothing I wanted to do more than slit this serial killer's neck more than he did to my brother. He did that to my brother before he shot him in the head. It was a quick death either way but I felt it was a pussy way to kill someone.

The next kill was someone in their bed. I didn't understand it and I knew they were taken by surprise. His neck was slit and it was done at sunset. It was a perfect time to escape. I knew I was thinking like the serial killer and getting inside his head. He had no time to fight back. If he would have had time to fight back he might have had some DNA under his fingernails or defensive wounds. He was a warrior and he was going to a better place. He didn't die right away and it was something that I respected. I was going to catch this serial killer for him. He was my warrior and I was going to get the guy who did this to him no matter what the cost was. If I had to die I was going to die catching the serial killer. I needed this to stop my drinking and drugs. My drug use was out of control and I stopped drinking. My drinking was gone and my cocaine was out of control. I was doing four big lines a day. It was out of control and I knew I needed to stop but I couldn't because I didn't know how. I was showing up high to work and the cops were noticing. I could still function but it wasn't one hundred percent. I was a mess and all this was separating me from the serial killer. I was away from the cases and the families that needed me to solve the cases. I was letting them down by not functioning at one hundred percent. I needed to stop this drug use and stop getting reality checks from the captain every time I came into work. I went into my martial arts class every day and practiced my fighting style. It was getting me fit to kick my drug habit to replace it with martial arts. It was working and I never did drugs again. I was sweating out all the drugs. I was doing well enough to impress the captain. I was still running out of breath and collapsing from all the drugs. It was a mess that I had to overcome. There was nothing I could do. I was getting overworked and it was good because I needed it. I was doing martial arts for three hours a day and they knew I was dedicated. It taught me self- defense and discipline. It taught me to believe in myself and he trusted me to get a hold of my life. It was like he knew me better than I knew myself. I told him more than I told most people because he was like family. I was going to my therapist and telling her about the serial killer I was chasing. She said I was going to catch him with the simplest clue. She said he was going to leave a clue behind by mistake when he meant to taunt us. I agreed and we talked about me being sober for three years without going to NA. We talked about martial arts and it was hard to distinguish between mental health and what it was like to have freedom if it was all gone. It was a great way to maintain a way of good mainstream discipline. I was going to go every day and fight my instructor for a challenge. It was nice to have a change of fighting students and the instructor on different days. I loved fighting other students because I was just as good as them. I was there for three years and they were there for ten years and it was great fighting them. It was so fun fighting and when we were busting drug dealers we were fighting hand to hand. Some of them were really good fighters and this was where the training came in. I was good at fighting and I wanted to fight in real life but it wasn't going to happen. I was going to use my self- defense for good and not to kill people. I was going to use it to arrest people and that was it. I was practicing at the martial arts center with my teacher. It was nice when it was just me and him. He told me her first and last name after all this time and it was a sign of respect. I was in love with her and we started dating and it was a love that was unbreakable. I was head over heels for her and she loved me for who I was. She and I had occasional drinks together at restaurants. We went to expensive restaurants once a month and we loved each other enough to get married. After a year she was good enough to introduce to the family. We needed each other and we were good enough to make each other happy. We made people around us happier and my family started talking to me again. After I started dating her my family changed and wanted me to visit them once a week. They finally realized I wasn't the bad guy. I was not alone anymore and I was happy to find someone that completed me and made me whole again. She completed me and if I lost her I would give up on love. We liked the same things and I would bring her home to the family once a week because they loved her. I was proud to show her to the family because she was beautiful, smart and she had an amazing job. If she ever got in trouble she knew how to defend herself. I was good at knowing my limitations and I knew not to drink or do drugs anymore. I hardly drank anymore and if I did I drank very little. I drank one or two drinks and I had it well under control. We were going steady and we were seeing good movies and holding hands. We were both cops and we were both looking for the serial killer. We knew it was a difficult battle that was all uphill. We were great at catching serial killers and then we were put in the same division. We were partners and we couldn't have been happier. We were in the same division and seeing a lot of each other and hoping we didn't get in fights. We didn't get in fights and we had the perfect marriage while being great at communication. We were good at talking to each other about our feelings and we had no secrets. We both had our lovers but that didn't stop us from sharing how many partners we had in the past. We were honest about how many partners we had and I didn't tell her I had slept with hookers. I was going to say that she was understanding that I slept with them. I was going to take it to my grave because I feared if I told her she would have a broken heart. We all had to have our secrets and I was sure she had her secrets and I wanted to know them but I didn't need to know them. I was going to go for a walk to clear my head. I heard shots from the house. I went into the house and there was an intruder. The cops were called and he tried to steal her purse. She was stabbed and was rushed to the hospital. A couple more inches to the left and she would have bled out. It was a random attack and it was nothing that was to suggest it was the twenty cents killer. He was still killing and my girlfriend requested to get off the case. They let her off the case and I felt that was odd. She said she didn't want to see too much of me. She didn't want to get worn out and I thought that was a good idea. It was a good idea and I would have done the same thing if I was her. I would have liked to work a different serial killer job and catch serial killer after a couple of months. I couldn't go on after a couple of months. Catch killers and rapists and pedophiles and all that. I was good at that. I had been chasing her for twenty years already I mean I was forty eight already. There was nothing I had done that was catching this serial killer. It was frustrating all the cops I was working with and it was frustrating me. I was getting mad because I was doing nothing right. There was nothing to do but keep waiting for the next case hoping that there was evidence that would help us catch him. I was going to go crazy trying to catch him.

The next kill he made was a soccer player visiting his family and it was sad that he had to die and it was going to happen sooner or later. I wasn't sad because I hated soccer. Soccer was a stupid sport, it was boring, I didn't know how the time worked in professional soccer. I mean it was popular in Europe and it wasn't catching on in the U.S. I didn't think but whatever. I was guessing he was in his thirties. It was sad that his family had lost their son and it was going to be a bad loss for them and it was going to be a big funeral hopefully. They might have been a big family but I didn't know because I didn't know them. It was in the past now. Life is worth more than who we are and it's who we become as a person and what we make of ourselves. We can be successful and make a life for ourselves or we can do nosedives and be failures. It is all up to us. It is all who we are as people. We are who we are in this world and my dad taught me that. I don't know if I've ever been good enough in everyone else's mind but I didn't care what everyone else thought. They were going to think what they were going to think no matter what I did and that wasn't going to change. They were just cold hearted people sometimes and it seemed like there were people that didn't care about other people's feelings. I was going to feel like a jerk when I was going to take a walk by myself. I wasn't going to take my girlfriend because she didn't like taking walks. She was walking with me all the time and she was always with me talking with me. I wouldn't change that for the world. She was always giving me advice on how to control my anger and get things under control. It was nice because I had a lot of anger when it came to trying to catching this serial killer and she calmed me down when I needed it. She knew what to say when I was upset and that was just what I needed. I was learning to respect her more and more and she was my life outside of work. She knew me better than I knew myself and I didn't think that was possible. There was nothing that was going to slow me down on working on this case. I was working nonstop without any vacation time and that was stressful on me and my wife. She was promoted to captain of her department. She was making the money and I was jealous and I needed that money. I was needing a pay raise because I was getting paid shit. I was getting paid nothing for my efforts and I was nothing more than a petty cop. I was nothing more than a cop that couldn't catch a criminal that was smarter than him. I was getting outsmarted and losing his cool. I had nothing left in the tank and retirement was tight around the corner. Sixty was retirement and it was right around the corner. It was probably going to be when I was going to be when I was going to catch this serial killer. Sixty was twelve years away and I was waiting until sixty four to retire whether I caught the serial killer or not. He was elusive and smart and trained by the other serial killer. He was the worst kind of serial killer and he had definitely killed more people than the other twenty cents killer. There was nothing that was going to catch this serial killer other than the serial killer himself. He was too smart and he was going to get caught when he wanted to get caught and he told me that in a letter. He was going to be a good killer for years to come and it was going to be a time when forensics was going to have come a long way from five years ago. It had come a long way in the last ten years and fingerprints were a huge deal where they weren't used in the seventies. It wasn't even heard of in the seventies because it didn't exist. DNA didn't exist back then either and it had come a long way too. I wanted DNA at the crime scenes to and it wasn't going to happen. There was nothing to go on and I was coming home in a bad mood most nights. My wife Sarah gave me a massage like most nights and asked how work went. It was a bad night at work and it was more people that ended up dead.

It was a family of five that ended up dead. It was a tragedy that they were all stabbed to death. The teenagers were stabbed to death first and then the parents. He left with some jewelry but I don't think he really wanted the jewelry. It was jewelry worth ten thousand dollars and it was a pretty good getaway and it was good living for him. There was nothing that was right about this family's stabbings. There was a lot of blood at the crime scene and it was estimated that they died at 1:30a.m. which was really early and it was something that was a surprise for them all. They were taken by surprise and it was a massacre. He was stabbing a lot lately so we figured he must have had a lot of rage. He was angry so we thought he was releasing rage from stabbing. There was perfume in the air and there was no perfume in the house. We were dealing with a female serial killer. It was a serial killer that was female and we tied her to all the crimes and we all agreed. It was a female serial killer and we noticed it and some other crime scenes too. It wasn't just at this crime scene it was at four other crime scenes as well that there was female perfume in the air. It was strong in the air and it was like she sprayed it in the air. It was twilight brand from a store in a nearby mall. We knew it was because one of the cops smelled it and bought it for his mom. It also came in lotion and bath bubbles for ten bucks. It was a package deal and it was a pretty good deal. I was sure the serial killer sprayed the perfume to let us know she was a female. I got a note from the serial killer and it was chilling and I read it and did as she said.

"I'm sure you know by now that I am a female serial killer and that I sprayed the twilight female brand perfume. I know this because I had a microphone in the house. You are right on the brand of perfume and I am a female serial killer. Print in the paper that you are looking for a female serial killer or I will kill another one of your family members."

I had the papers print that we were looking for a female serial killer and that we had got the information from a perfume sprayed at the last crime scene. She was satisfied enough not to kill another one of my family members. I was happy about that and I slept better at night. My girlfriend read in the paper that we were looking for a female serial killer and she was quite intrigued. She was going to have sex with me tonight. We had sex three times a week and she was thirty seven and I was forty eight. We had a kid and we were happy we had a girl named Shelby. Shelby was a beautiful girl and she weighed eight ounces when she was born and she was a big baby when she was born. She was the light of our life in a dark world of trying to catch a serial killer that could be after us next. We could always have a target over our heads and that was scary. We were afraid for our lives because so many of our family members had died and we were lucky that more of our family members hadn't died and we were going to take many vacations when we retired. There was nothing we liked more than spending time with little Shelby. She was a bundle of joy and she was growing up so fast and before we knew it she was five. She was very playful and I got hit by a car and it was going to be a recovery time of six weeks and it was going to be paid vacation of three weeks. The bills were paid for by Sarah because she made enough money for the both of us. She was making twice as much money as I was. I was going through a hard time with getting addicted to my pills. I got addicted to cocaine and then I was going to AA. I quit AA and started becoming an alcoholic. I quit altogether and I was going to quit forever. I wasn't going to drink again because I was just addicted to pills and it was just from my broken leg that I got addicted to those pills. I was going to catch this serial killer and that's all I had on my mind and he was going to admit his guilt. If he didn't confess we had nothing. I was going to make him confess if it was the last thing I did. I was the best at making people confess even if I had to get a little rough with them. There was nothing wrong with getting a little rough with them as long as you didn't hurt them. Just put them against the wall and intimidate them into confessing. They were all guilty if you knew it and you knew beyond a shadow of a doubt that they were guilty. I was going to catch her and it was going to be easy once I did. I was going to be old because I already felt old. I was going to be the only cop to do it because all these cops were amateurs. They didn't know what they were doing but then again I didn't know what I was doing either. I wasn't catching her either. There was an unmistakable feeling that my family should have been protected better but they were so far away and I could have protected my brother more. I could have let my brother stay with me but he still would have died unless he would have come home before me. It was a nightmare and I would wake up in sweat. We moved because people would break in armed and we would have to kill them and call the cops. We moved with no more break ins. I was sleeping better at night because without any break-ins I didn't have to worry about protecting Sarah or Shelby. There was nothing I wanted more than to protect my family. We were working out at the dojo and we were practicing take downs and practicing how to take away knives and guns. We were practicing real life situations. She was trained in these situations and they were good things to know. I was impressed with how much she knew. I was going home with lots of knowledge and she was good at a lot of things. We were good at takedowns and we knew what we were doing. We went to take karate and kick boxing and we were going to know a lot of fighting skills. We were the best in our class at karate and kick boxing within a couple of years and it was nice. We were trained well and we had good students to fight. We were good at a lot of things and we were going to bars and drinking a couple of drinks. We were going to kid movies with our daughter and enjoying it.

We were just enjoying life and then my dad died from cancer. We went to his funeral and everyone showed up. It was a good turnout.

My mom had died a couple of years ago from breast cancer.

My aunt and uncle had died a year apart from lung cancer from smoking. My dad had been battling cancer for a couple of years. He had lost a couple of days ago and we had his funeral today. We had about a thirty people there and it was a decent turnout considering. There was nothing that I was going to say about him in front of everybody and I was shy to say anything. My cousin was there and we talked for a couple of minutes. I had gotten a couple of tattoos and it was showing on my forearms. They were song quotes and I also had three skulls on my wrist. I was loving my tattoos and I wouldn't explain them to anybody. My wife didn't even know what they meant and she knew everything about me. I wasn't going to tell her because she didn't need to know. Nobody needed to know besides me. I was a lone wolf and I was my own pack leader on this case. I was going to solve this case by myself. I was going to find this serial killer myself and she was going to go down for all these kills. She had killed seven thousand people and the numbers were going up. It was going to continue going up and I was going to catch her if it cost me my life and my job. I was going to give my life to this job and it was my career on the line here. I was going to try and find the evidence even if there wasn't any. I wasn't going to plant any evidence by any means or fabricate any evidence if there was any but it was going to make it hard to make to get any evidence if there was none. There was nothing I could do but wait for the next case. The next case was going to roll across the desk and I hoped she got sloppy which I knew she wouldn't do. There was nothing that she was doing that was amateur. She was a pro. I believed I was going to be retired by the time I caught her. I was going to have to sacrifice a lot to catch her and I got a tattoo that said deliver me from this place, deliver me oh lord. It was a song quote. It was a good song quote from a movie Cabin by the Lake and it is my favorite song in the world. I find it to be a quote like a lord's prayer. I was getting home from work and then I was going to the store for some milk.

There was a robbery and the cashier had a gun to his face and I shot the robber. He was thankful and I was happy to provide the service. I was just happy to get rid of the dirt bag. He was dead and I was thankful that the cashier didn't get shot. He was lucky he gave the money to the robber and I was glad that I was there. I was glad that I had brought my gun because I was thinking of leaving it at home but I take my gun everywhere. I thought since I was a cop I would take it into the store and no one would mind. I was lucky they allowed guns in the store. I was lucky that they didn't ask if I was a cop. I showed him I was a cop and then phoned it into the cops. They showed up and closed off the crime scene. I gave my statement, left and went home. I gave her the eggs and milk and she made waffles. We all ate a good breakfast at seven in the morning and it was very good blueberry waffles. I was eating cheesecake with the family and went to work.

We got a lead of a footprint at the scene and it was a woman's Nike size nine. It was very common and it was nothing we could track. We didn't have any witnesses who saw the killer. There was nothing we had to go on yet again and it was a bust and there was a lot of blood spatter on the clothes in the dumpster and it was very familiar clothing. There was nothing to tie it to the suspect. There was nothing that was going to tie anyone to this crime and I was mad once again. There was nothing to tie anyone to these crimes. I was mad we weren't catching this criminal. I was playing a lot of pool with Sarah and she was really good. She could make pool balls in by banking shots and I wasn't good at all. It was all for fun. I was getting better and finally beating her in a couple of games and we were going out a couple of nights a week. We were all going to eat and our daughter was nine and it was going smoothly. I was impressed with the serial killer even though she had left behind a shoeprint.

Then she had stomped a victim to death and that was the first time she had done that. It was just a horrible way to die. It was like a horrible dream for the family. It was like losing a baby of the family. It was like a piece of you was missing and it was like there was a piece of you that was taken away from you. There was nothing you wanted to do but ask the serial killer to take you instead of your child. The only thing you could do was remember your child for who they were and remember the good times you spent with them and live through them. It was going to be good times if you could learn to live with their memories and carry their memories with you. Their light was always going to shine in you and through you. Out of the darkness comes a light that they had all along that was always shined when they were alive. I was having fun and we were spending a lot of time at the park. We were taking a lot of walks and seeing a lot of nature. It was nice tanning weather. There was nothing that was better than getting outside and getting out and enjoying the great weather. Work was taking up most of our time and we were paying the babysitter. We were getting to stay up late and watching Netflix and it was mostly forensic files and criminal minds and numbers. We were up all night and going to work. We were getting six hours of sleep and it was a good weekend. We were working every day and it was getting to us. We were working long hours and it was just going to wear us out. It was going to get to us and get under our skin and not make us want to work ever again and when we retired we wouldn't have to. We were listening to our I Pods to sleep and we were snuggling. We were having good breakfasts like a good family. I was tired every day from long work hours and it was getting to me not catching this serial killer. and it was just like we were never going to catch this serial killer.

She was getting her kicks killing and now she was chopping up her bodies and it was a new thing for her. There was no end to this madness and eventually this was going to stop. If it wasn't we were just going to have to keep up. There was nothing we could do but keep up and keep investigating these sick chopped up murders. There was no murder that was going to go unsolved… eventually. We were going to nail her it was just a matter of when. I was going to go to the bar and play pool to cool off and then go for a walk by myself and cool off.

It was nice weather for a walk and I saw someone getting mugged. He had a gun and I used my martial arts skills and kick boxing training to disarm him. He ran away and I got back her purse and it was a good day. It was a good thing she was uninjured. It was just a thing where I had to help and I had heard her screaming. I had to help since I had the skills. She was thankful and paid me twenty dollars. I paid her the twenty dollars back and she bought me dinner. We were talking and she was a very nice girl. It was a nice dinner and I told her I was married and so was she. She had a couple of tattoos as did I and we explained what they were about. I realized I explained what my tattoos were about when I hadn't explained my tattoos to my wife who I told everything to. I was happy to have dinner with this girl because she was nice. I went home and I climbed into bed with my wife. We were just glad to spend some quality time together. We went to bed and we had another kid and named her Rose. It was nice and I was going to work and getting nowhere with this serial killer. It was going to be a long day and it was going to be no leads once again.

There was a murder and it was chopped up body

on the streets and it was an old couple and it was an old veteran that had fought in Korea and he was a true hero. His wife used to work at the post office. It was a noble job that she loved. She worked there for fifty years. There was a true worker and she was a hard worker from what her co-workers said. Her neighbors said she was the nicest lady and she was a good friend to them. I was thinking I was too old to work as a cop but then I had a serial killer to catch. I was going to catch him before I retired. I was going to retire as the cop that caught the twenty cent killer. I was going to be the hero. The perfume was the main clue and the shoeprint was the other main clue. Those were the main clues we had to work with. It was our anniversary coming up and it was going to be an expensive present coming for my wife. I got her a diamond bracelet and she got me a Rolex watch. We got the perfect gifts for each other and we were satisfied with these gifts. We couldn't have asked for anything more from each other. We were going about our business every day and we were going to work every day investigating crimes. We were cleaning up the streets and putting away drug dealers and pedophiles and people like that. There was nothing better than the feeling of putting away criminals and it was a feeling that you couldn't get from any other job. It was something that I was satisfied with.

I was going to go to bed when there was a string of robberies and murders. I got called to the scenes and it was gruesome and it was like they were committed within hours of each other. There was no sense to these murders. They could have been tied up and robbed, they didn't have to be murdered. This was just brutal and I couldn't take it I was mad and I couldn't contain my anger. I screamed and I just lost it at the crime scene. They had to calm me down and they had never seen me this mad. It was a side to me that was getting to be out of control and they were all mad. They didn't let it show like I did and it was like they didn't care how much he killed anymore. I was a useless cop that wasn't ever going to catch this serial killer. I felt alone investigating this serial killer. I felt like everyone else had given up on these cases and I had run out of things to say to these families. It was hard to talk to these families that had lost loved ones. Loved ones could never be replaced and it was going to be hard to explain to the kids that they were never going to see their dad again. I had kids and if they lost me to the murderer I didn't know how my wife was going to explain it to the children. The children were going to be heartbroken and it was going to be hard on them. It was going to be like a knife to the heart to them. I was going to be a rock for them. I was going to be there for them for a long time. I was going to be there for them through graduation and marriage and see them do good things. I was going to be there for them when they needed me through the good times and bad. It was bad enough I had lost so many family members to the serial killer and it was still hard to take after all these years. There was a hurt that was still there. It had been replaced by many years of drinking and drugs and now I had replaced it with a great wife. I had waited for so long and God had answered my prayers. He had given me a gift and I wasn't going to waste it this time around. There was a good thing that I had and I was going to cherish it for the rest of our lives. There was an aching feeling that the serial killer wanted to get to know me and pick my brain and make me go crazy. He was going to make me go crazy and he was already making me go crazy and I had been chasing him for so long. It had been twenty five years I had been chasing him and I was fifty three. It wasn't making me look too old for the department. Some of the original people working the case had retired. They brought in fresh eyes and they were twenty two and twenty four year olds. There was nothing wrong with that because we needed young blood.

We had a double homicide and it was a young couple that had been scuba diving off the coast of Aruba. They came back according to friends and then they were killed. It was just odd they were killed after that. It was just like the killer knew they had just came back from vacation. I was baffled and I was just at a loss for words. This serial killer had killed recent honeymooners and it was just another tragedy. It was like he knew they were coming back to visit family after vacation and it was going to be a long investigation into these murders. There was nothing that was going to be easy to solve these cases and it was going to get me mad when I figured out who was the serial killer. I would figure it out and he would leave that clue that would make me know who he was. He would make a mistake and I would catch.

I was sleeping when there was a murder and it was another cop and he got shot in the head and it was a black cop. He was killed under a bridge. It was a married cop and his wife was at the crime scene crying. She identified him under the sheet when the coroner pulled it back. There was no denying he was a good cop and he was investigating a drug ring. There was a drug ring in the city that was getting kids addicted to drugs and then getting them to be drug dealers. That was the life and it was just the way it went. There was a prostitution ring in the city and we busted the culprit and he went away for twenty years and that stopped and it was all shutdown and I was pretty satisfied. My wife and I went to play pool and we were getting better. I won and we both went home and watched football. We always cheered on the Vikings. I was going to wait for hell to freeze over for a Minnesota to win a championship of some kind.

Now another college basketball player died and it was no surprise that he was a decent player. He was going to be a first round pick for the NBA and it was going to be an honor to have our school have a player go to the NBA especially the first round. There was a lot of players that went to the NBA but none of them from our school went to the NBA. Now it was time to get something going and see if there were any clues and there wasn't like usual. I wasn't getting anywhere and I was spinning my wheels. I needed clues to solve these cases and I wasn't getting them. I was becoming older every day that I wasn't catching this serial killer and he was laughing at me. I wasn't going to have the serial killer laughing at me when I caught her and I was going to catch her soon. I was dreaming bad dreams and I was hoping those dreams were going to go away. I was having good meals and taking care of my kids. I was watching them grow up before my eyes. I was working ten hours a day looking for a serial killer with no results. It was like I was spinning my wheels and I was going to find her eventually. I was going to make detective in a couple of weeks and have a new team. It was going to be nice having a new team.

I was going to get paid a little more and that was going to be nice. I was going to be in a new office and I was still going to be investigating the serial killer. I was going to make it big when I caught this serial killer and the other detectives were going to be doing something else. The other detectives in my office were going to be doing something else. I was going to be the only one investigating the serial killer. I was going to be the one to catch this serial killer and I was going to be the one to get the job of finding the evidence. I was getting the letters and being told to keep them to myself. It was like the serial killer knew me. It was like the serial killer wanted to get to know me better. It was hitting me close to home with these letters and she was telling me what type of people she was going to kill next. I was okay with that and she was tainting my detecting skills. It was like a cat and mouse game and I liked games. Games were my specialty. I was waiting for my turn to get my shot at the drug dealers and see if they knew about the serial killer which I knew they wouldn't. One of them sold to the serial killer and they wouldn't give a description because she was a regular. She would use with him and he never gave up his customers. He said her name was Sarah. It was a good start and I was quite intrigued that he gave up that much and I was just curious who this Sarah was. It was his side of the story but later he said it was a lie. There was nothing that they did that was better than that to them. They weren't bothered by anyone and the cops never busted this drug dealer. He had never been arrested for anything. He was very smart in the way he sold drugs and he could sniff out the cops. He knew a cop from a buyer. He knew when the cops were watching and where they were at all times.

I was called to the scene of a couple that had

their heads chopped off. it was a lot of blood and they were in their beds. It was blood all over in their beds. it was just like they were positioned in a certain way. They were positioned in a suggestive way and they were sleeping. They didn't have a chance to defend themselves.

I was at home in a couple of hours after there was another kill. It was a construction worker that was laid off for the winter and he was working at Wal- Mart. It was a job that he didn't like and it was a job that he had to work to make a little extra money. He was single and it was just something he had to do until he got that call back. Now he was never going to get that call and his boss showed up to the funeral. I was a big believer that construction workers were one of the hardest workers that I knew. They had to be very strong and they had to have a lot of upper body strength and work out a lot. They were going to work a lot of hours and you couldn't work on rainy days I don't think. I was a big believer in thinking that you had to be a good worker and work in construction as a career and not a job. Most people had it as a career and my cousin loved it. He was so rich he owned a house, a hunting lodge and a few other houses. There was nothing he couldn't have because he had that much money. It was ridiculous and life wasn't about money but I wish I had that much money. I wanted to be that well off and be able to provide for my family like that. I was watching T.V. when I heard a knock at the door and it was the captain.

He said there was a decapitation at a house and it was bloody. It was a teenager and he had been babysitting a kid and the kid was still alive. He was watching T.V. and it was still on and the kid was screaming. There was no way that the parents could come home to this and we sealed the crime scene off. It was a babysitter and the kid was about three and I was baffled that the serial killer could do this and I was sad for this this teenager. He didn't deserve to die this way and I was going to find this serial killer and get justice for him and all the other victims. I wanted to kill this serial killer no matter who this serial killer was. It was sad that this serial killer was still out there after twenty five years. It was a long time and I wanted to catch her more than ever and twenty five years was too long for any serial killer. There was no way this serial killer was going to kill until I retired because I wasn't going to let her. I was losing my edge because I wanted this drug dealer to give me a sketch of the serial killer. I knew he knew what she looked like and it was frustrating. It was like he was toying with us. I was getting tired of him toying with us and I gave up on him giving us a sketch of our serial killer. It was like we were never catch this serial killer without that sketch but we would find other ways. I was going to find the evidence and it was going to come eventually. There was going to be evidence eventually and he was going to give us that sketch if we gave him something in return. I was going blind looking at these case files especially these case files regarding these beheadings. It was brutal and it was a new thing for this serial killer. I was getting drunk at the bars once in a while because Sarah was coming home late most nights. She was hanging out with friends most of those nights. I was taking care of the kids and she was working late. It was a late night and she was tired from work. We were always having fun one way or another and then we both got shot. We were both lying there wondering what to do. The next day we were going to work and having a babysitter come to the house. It was nice only having to pay the babysitter two hundred dollars a week. We paid a little extra and she was a nice girl and very pretty for her age. She was eighteen and I suspected my wife was cheating on me and I was definitely suspecting it. I was going to be pretty pissed if she was. I was going to get over it if she was. We would work it out by going to marriage counseling and it would be fine.

Now it was a murder of a librarian and it was an older librarian and she was about fifty five and she was dead from a stab wound to the chest. There was nothing to suggest that we were going to find the murder weapon but then again we found it in the dumpster outside the library. It was covered with blood all over the blade. There were no fingerprints on the handle and it looked like from the testing it was all the victim's blood on the blade. It was a case where there was no evidence to tie anything to the serial killer. It was something that was a regular thing for me. The librarian was just a regular person that didn't have to die like anyone else. It was just like she had died the way she lived, living a normal life. She died with a book in her hand and I thought that was cool. She went out doing what she loved doing, reading a book and drinking coffee. She loved cats and dog. She had called her daughter the night before wishing her a happy birthday. She was 55 with her own apartment in Riverside park and it was a nice place. It was a big apartment for seven hundred dollars a month and it was a good price. There was a lot of crying at the funeral and it was going to be a tough time for everyone. I was getting tired of all the crime scenes murders and beheadings. It was all brutal and it was one kill after another. The death toll was eight thousand. This was the most kills in history and no one had seen this much killing ever. There was nothing that could be done to done to stop this serial killer. I wasn't getting much sleep since my baby Shelby and it was and it would wake up the baby and it was a vicious cycle. It was a nightmare and then it would affect Rose's schoolwork where she would be a straight A student but then when she got used to it she would be a straight A student without my help. It was nice that way and she was very smart. She was very dedicated and everything came easy to her. She was like a whiz kid and it was like nothing was hard for her to understand.

It was winter again and the serial killer was chopping up the bodies and putting them in hockey arenas. It was like he wanted multiple people to find the body. It was obvious the body was planted and she was killed somewhere else. It was going to be a mystery to figure out where the person was killed. It didn't matter because it still wouldn't tell us who the serial killer was. There was no point in thinking where the murder took place. There were about ten more cops at the crime scene with me and they all wondering where she was killed. I was thinking why the hell did it matter? It wasn't going to tell us who the serial killer was so stop thinking about it and get it out of your mind. There was no point in thinking about it because it wasn't going to do any of us any good. Now there was going to be another kill.

Sure enough there was a kill in a park where families took their kids. There was a body in the sand and some kid had tripped over an arm. It was sticking up out of the ground. I was called to the crime scene with five other cops. It was closed off for a couple of minutes and then the body was carefully dug up. The temperature was taken and the time of death was midnight to three a.m. The body was hauled off to the coroners cooler.

Then there was another kill and the body was in the woods and it was close to a walking trail. It was discovered by a few joggers. It was a female jogger and it was recognized by her neighbors. It was lucky they were jogging that day. They were out that day with thick clothes on a cold twenty degree day. It was a negative degree windshield but they didn't care. They jogged every day because it was their morning routine. Most people walked the mall and jogged this trail for five miles there and back. It was their morning routine. They headed home and did it one more time. They thought of what they did to type their one book together. It was a romantic novel and it was a book that my wife would read because she loved romantic novels. She always watched lifetime movies because we had Direct TV. She loved life time TV and she could watch that all day. We also had Hulu and we loved that as well. There was a lot of things that we had. There were things that we wanted like our family members back and there was a serial killer that I needed to catch to end my career. There was nothing that I loved more than forensics or work a regular cop job. I wanted to be a detective somewhere else. I was sick of this serial killer and I needed to catch this serial killer for my family. I wanted them to truly love me again because they had hate in their hearts even if they didn't say it. I was mad I couldn't catch this serial killer because I was working so hard with no results. I was going to catch her. I wasn't thinking it was a guy and being wrong. If it wasn't for that perfume at that crime scene I would have thought it was a guy. I would have still been wrong after all these years. I had too much pressure on my shoulders catching this serial killer. Everyone wanted results now. They wanted me to catch the serial killer every day and they thought that today was the day. Today was going to be the day I was going to catch him and that just wasn't the case. I wasn't going to catch the serial killer the way the captain wanted me to. I was going to catch her on my terms and that was how I was going to operate. I was going to get down and dirty and get my feet wet. I was going to get the wheels turning and get some evidence somewhere. There was going to be some evidence that the serial killer was going to leave behind eventually. They all leave behind evidence eventually. This killer has killed and left behind shoe impressions. We had a name and that was something. We had so many things to help this case but it wasn't adding up to anything. She had changed her killing style so many times that it was ridiculous. It was like she was getting comfortable with different killing styles. Killing styles changed but people never did. It was like she was changing everything about herself. She was a cunning killer and from my view she was charismatic. It was like she knew her way around every sort of weapon. I was impressed with her weapon selection.

She had used a chainsaw according to our weapons expert and it was like she liked using every sort of weapon she could get her hands on. She was using a chainsaw to chop up her bodies. She was leaving them in various places and it was places that were where people could see them. It was where people could easily spot them. I was going to take a day off from work and spend some time with my kids. That was going to be my day and I was going to have a fun day. My work didn't let me do that. They had me come in and that was a drag and they wouldn't let me do that unless I was horribly sick. I wasn't getting off that easily and I went to the bank. I had some errands to run and my wife had another late night at work. It was what the usual, a tweaker she had to put away. A meth lab she had to take care of and a drug dealer she busted. She was getting a lot of work done. She was going to get things done and it was like she was wonder woman. It was like she was all these places at once. It was like she was a one woman show. She was the only woman doing her job while the other cops sat around on their asses eating donuts and did nothing. There was nothing to do at work but try and find out how the serial killer ticked. There was a few drug busts here and there but it was boring. There was something that was bothering me, why was the serial killer changing her killing style? She was killing all these different people leaving them in all these different places and it was weird.

I found a former marine that was working at Target that trespassed on an army base. It was weird because the serial killer wanted us to find him in this ironic place. It was weird and I didn't want to begin to understand this. It was just weird that all these marines called it in because he was retired and wasn't in the army. He was a civilian and that was what I found to be the strangest part. It was ironic to find him here and we investigated it like any other case. He was missing his head and all his fingers and there was no way to identify him. He had a few tattoos and we didn't want to have his family look at him and identify him because he had no head. We had his tattoos in the paper and then his family came in and identified them and said that was their son. That was the end of it and they had him cremated. He was put in their home and it was nice for him to be in a safer place. He was remembered as a nice guy and he had a closed casket funeral with a few people in the family. A few people showed up and it was a turnout that the army would have been proud of. There were family members from all over the state that came with tears running down their faces. His name was Jared and he was a true marine when he was in the army. He was a good fighter and a true warrior with a lot of action in Iraq. He had fought in Iraq a lot and had done four tours. He had been there for ten years and he was tired of all the fighting. He had retired and he was the fighter that his squad had wanted him to be. He had killed a few people was sick of pulling the trigger on little kids. He had got the mission done for all the war heroes out there. There was all the stupid things that were all so simple to fight about in this country. It may seem simple to you but to other countries it seems complicated.

Money is hard to comprehend to some countries and we are lucky we aren't a poor country. Some are suffering and we are complaining about stupid stuff. We were still over in Iraq after all these years and there were no signs of pulling out after killing Osama Bin Ladin and capturing Sudam Hussein. There was no end and the only reason we were there was to try and get their army situation figured out. I say they can figure it out themselves. If they have to rely on us all the time they won't learn anything. They will never learn to fight for themselves and they will always depend on someone else if it isn't us. There will never be an end to getting out of Iraq. Iraq sucks and I want our troops out or we will stay forever. There was never a good idea to go in the first place and everyone thought it was a good idea to go. Oh this is such a good idea they told Bush and now look at us it blew up in our face. When we were there too long it was suddenly George Bush's fault. No it was our fault for suggesting the idea of going.

There was a killing of a college football player on a football field. He was killed with a gunshot to the head. There was no way of knowing who he was. We had an idea after asking the coach. He suggested one player was missing on the team and that was the idea that we needed. We called the parents and they had a closed casket for him. He was remembered for who he was. His parents had a couple of words to say and then he was buried. There was heartache and then he was buried and then there was another case. The whole police force forgot about him and moved onto the next case.

The next case was a serial killer and he was stabbed with a knife to the back of the head in his apartment. He was suspected in several crimes and he was about to be arrested. He got killed before we could arrest him but it was justice either way. There was nothing we could do to catch him before the serial killer got to him. The serial killer was in his thirties and was a creepy looking guy with a beard and mustache. It was pretty clear that he lived alone and I knew he was going to die alone because he stayed out all hours of the night. He never had any interest at having a girlfriend or wife. There was nothing that he liked doing for hobbies because he was never home to take care of pets or anything like that. It was a public service that this serial killer would take care of this other serial killer because he had also raped ten other woman. There was no doubt this serial killer that was killed was depraved when he raped. He had raped more than ten but they had gotten away. They didn't get a good look at him but we knew it was him. Now that we had come close to catching him. We werent sad that he was killed because like every serial killer he only thought about himself and not his actions.

The next kill on this serial killer's list was a released pedophile. It was a woman and it was a good deed for this serial killer. She had been raping five year old boys and it was a bad thing. She was just depraved and she needed to be killed. It was like she needed to rape little boys to get her sick kicks. She was the lowest scum of the Earth. She was going to die in prison or by someone else. She died by the serial killer's hand and it was another public service. I was glad she died and it was me smiling inside. There was nothing that made me happier and then there was another pedophile that died. His three best friends were gone and they were nowhere in sight. It wasn't unlikely that the serial killer would have done this. If the last pedophile was a guy she probably would have done the same thing. It was not like her to kill pedophiles. It was her first and second time killing a pedophile and that was striking to me. It was not like her to kill someone different like this so late in the game. It didn't matter in the end because some of these people were scum and deserved to die.

The next kill she made was a sports announcer and he was covering college games. He was about sixty seven and he was quite frequent on the college games. It was sad to see him die because he was one of the best college announcers I had ever heard. He was a good announcer and he would be missed. I always loved his announcing because he was so colorful and full of statistics. When a college game was being played he would always give you the best statistics about every player on the team. He was the best play by play announcer. He was the best announcer in my mind and he was going to be missed by everyone that knew him. I was going to miss him and I went to his funeral and it was about ten miles away. There were going to be a lot of people there and with a lot of people crying. He was going to have a lot of family members saying kind words. I said a few kind words about him and I was going to say a few things about him in memory. I was going to throw a few black roses on his grave that I had been color dyed. I was saddened by his loss. We had a few players that went into the NBA because of him and it was nice that way. It was going to be nice that this announcer had got offered to announce for the NBA. He had turned it down because he had grown up here and he wanted to stay true to his roots. He wanted to be a simple man and be true to his fans. He didn't want to leave the simple life. He had the life, announcing for a college basketball team. I would have taken the NBA job but he wanted to stay with his hometown. He didn't want to leave his fans and he wanted to stay where he knew he could please the people. He didn't want the change of scenery and I could understand that. We had lost a very good announcer and no announcer would ever fill his shoes. It would never be the same. I wasn't going to watch college basketball anymore because he had died. We had a lot of loyal fans that were going to stop coming to the games. They were dedicated to the announcer who died and his name was Bob and he was great. He was the guy that made college basketball fun to watch. I was living in the moment when I was watching every college basketball game. I was glued to the T.V. and that wasn't going to happen anymore. The college basketball fans diminished by ten percent for ticket fans. People stopped watching and then they didn't want to watch without their favorite announcer. There was nothing worth watching without their favorite announcer and it was like the Bert and Ernie world was destroyed.

The next kill was a volunteer firefighter and he was set on fire. It was with gasoline in the middle of the street and no one wanted to say anything. If he was willing to do that he was willing to kill anyone that was willing to get in his way. It was someone with a hood according to witnesses. I think he did it to scare people and intimidate people. People were afraid because if he was willing to do this he was willing to shoot someone execution style in the head in a bar. That was the best that we could get. It was someone with a mask on according to another person. It was all going to shit and it was all something that was a different story. We had several different stories and it wasn't panning out to anything. It was nothing that we could use. We had another witness that said the assailant was five eight and it was useful. I was going on that and it wasn't much to put pen to paper. It didn't lead to much. There was nothing we had to go on and there was nothing that was happening in these cases that was generating any leads. There were all these people calling in asking when we were going to catch this serial killer. The thing was we didn't know when we were going to catch this serial killer. When we did he was going to have a lot of kills under her belt.

She was going to have more than ten thousand kills under her belt. She had eleven thousand under her belt right now and we had no intention of telling the media that. There was nothing the media wouldn't sniff out. They were cadaver dogs when it came to these sort of things. I was frustrated because I didn't know how one can one serial killer kill eleven thousand people. It was ridiculous and I had no response for the victims. There were all of these cases on my old desk and it was getting to me. There was nothing I could do about it and my wife didn't want me to drink. There was no way to forget about it. My health was declining from all the years of drinking and drugs. I was in no shape to catch this serial killer because she was killing so many people.

He was setting people on fire and chopping off their heads. We weren't able to identify some of these bodies. These victims weren't getting a proper burial and it was a bad thing for the families. There were so many people missing their loved ones. We didn't know which ones were the right victim's to the right families and it was really concerning us. The serial killer was making so many people disappear in one day. It was hard to figure out which family member's kids belonged to who. After a while and we didn't know where to look. We didn't know where the kids were because the serial killer never kidnapped kids. This was a new thing for her. She was burying them somewhere but the question was where. We had no answers for the parents. The parents were coming in and asking what we were doing to find their children and we told them we were investigating all leads. The truth was we had no leads and we weren't looking for anything to go on. We were tired of searching for leads. We were looking for the serial killer on current cases. All we could do was work on current cases. We were jumping on current cases. We were in a blender being mixed up and being mashed together. With all these ingredients there was nothing that was being contributed. There were all these variables coming into play and we had to deal with all of them. If we were going to solve this case I needed to figure in all the variables and leads. I was on my knees praying to God that I solve this case soon. I was praying that I catch this serial killer before she killed another thousand people. There was a madness to her and she was dangerous to every family. She was destroying every life she touched. There was nothing she wasn't destroying. I was like a fractured ankle, I couldn't play when it was crunch time and the team really needed me. There was no real threat to the family. When the serial killer was after them it was like nothing else mattered. She was never going to come after me because she needed me and she liked me being in control with me in the driver's seat. She was harmless to my family even with the break ins. They were unrelated to the serial killer. There was no relation to the serial killer and the break-ins in my house were so stupid because he didn't want me to be scared of him. The serial killer wanted me to know she wasn't going to come after me because her and I had a connection that was like no other. Without me she couldn't put on a show. I was her audience as crazy as that sounds and she needed an audience to perform in front of. She was putting a show for me and she needed me because she was showing off. I was her favorite cop and she wanted me to be the lead detective on this case. She said that in one of her letters. She was quite open in her letters and said she wanted to meet me one day. She said we had met in passing and I had not known this. This intrigued me and I had to know where we had met. Then it hit me, we could have met in an in elevator or on the street. That was the only place that I could think or maybe in the waiting room of the place where we sit for my therapist appointment. That could have been it because I meet a lot of people there. That was probably it and I was going to find out who she was. It was going to take a couple of years but it was going to happen. It all seemed like a dream and I was hanging around the pool hall drinking. I was getting drunk playing pool and playing pretty good. I was playing a better pool player, where he was banking off the rails. I won with her having five balls on the table. I went home with a cab and picked the car up and drove home. I went to work and Sarah had another late night at work. I expected she was having an affair. I asked her about it and she said no and I believed her. She had no reason to lie to me and I always believed her because she never had a reason to lie. It was like I needed a drink again and Sarah frowned on me drinking but I was a big man and I could drink. I was going to drink if I wanted to and I could be a drunk if I wanted. I still suspected that she wasn't working late. She couldn't be working late all the time but I didn't know where she worked. I didn't want to follow her to work because I would be late to work. I was going to have to believe her at some point but I didn't want to because there was something going on that I didn't know about. There was something that she wasn't telling me and I wanted to know what it was. There was something she was keeping from me and I wanted to know what it was. We had no secrets and this was different.

The next kill was a hooker and she was very pretty. She was going to college full time according to her parents. She was hooking part time and it was like she was a bad girl trying to make good. There was nothing wrong with that. It sounded like she was trying to go straight and she wanted to better herself. She wanted to be a news anchor and there was nothing wrong with that. There was high praise from her parents for her trying to make a better life for herself. She was a couple of months in and it was going good career for her. She was getting good grades and she was attending school every day. She was making good money and supporting herself. She was a good college student in a college town. Everything was planned out and there was nothing she was doing that was getting her in trouble. She had no criminal record and she wasn't getting high or drunk. The good die young and the bad live forever. Now the bad like this serial killer have been killing for twenty five years and it's mindboggling. I was hard on myself and I was a good cop when it came to catching other serial killers that left behind clues and evidence. This serial killer wasn't leaving anything behind. I was getting tired of her killing good people and me having to tell the families that we were doing everything that we could to try and catch this serial killer. We were trying to catch her with no success. We had nothing so we couldn't do anything. We were in a small gopher hole trying to catch the gopher and we weren't having any success. There was nothing we could do and I was getting mad because there was nothing to go on. I was watching LeBron James blow the series against Golden State. He was going to lose the whole thing and it was going to be a disappointment. There was nothing that was going to be good about this.

It was a cold winter and we found a snow removal worker face down in the snow with a gunshot to the head. His truck was still running in the middle of the street. It was tragic for his kids and his wife. The town that was relying on the rest of the roads to have salt on the roads because he didn't even start on the roads. He was killed before he could start. The killer was smart to kill him to when he was about to pull out from the sidewalk. It was going to be a major loss to the snow removal company but they would find someone else. The family would be hit hard because the stay at home mom would have to pay for daycare. They would have to scrape by for money and it was going to be hard for her to find a decent paying job and pay for daycare. There wasn't a decent paying job for one person that could pay for daycare. It was like two hundred dollars a week and that was expensive. It was going to put a dent into the funds. I wondered how they were going to make it unless they got help from government food stamps and government aid. That was the only way they were going to make it. I was going to be surprised if they were going to keep the apartment. They had three kids that were two three and five. They were going to need to be baby sitters and it was going to be a lot of money to take care of them. There was going to be a lot of day care involved and they were going to spend a lot of money.

The next kill was a biker and he was killed

on his way to Sturgis. He was killed on a major highway and I find it ironic he was killed on his way to Sturgis and he had ten miles to go. He looked like a biker. He had the biker beard and mustache and the bandana with the sunglasses. He was riding with bikers that were killed and he was the one that got killed with a headshot. Like the others and it was all the serial killer but the others went missing so we didn't know if they were dead. They were suspected to be dead but we didn't know. We were suspecting they were buried somewhere and we were looking for them. It was going to be a long time before we were going to find them.

The next kill was an anchor and she was an anchor I had watched often. I watched the news and she was on at night and she was good. She was the reason I watched the news. They were going to have to find a good replacement because I wanted to watch a different news station. I watched the news every day. I watched sports center and it was what I fell asleep to and I left it all night. I was sleeping on the couch and it was more comfortable than the bed. It was going better now that Sarah was working later. We weren't having sex as much as we should. We were having sex in the mornings and it was good but it was quickies. the baby would wake every time we had sex. I was having an affair and I was suspecting my wife was doing the same. My affair was hotter than my wife and my wife told me she was having an affair. I told her I was doing the same and we vowed we would never do it again. We didn't do it anymore and we knew we had to be faithful. We knew it was something that we were ashamed that we did but that was all in the past. We never meant for it to happen but like addictions we couldn't stop and when we did we knew we couldn't do it anymore. We broke off the affair and got back to having sex with each other and we were happy again. We were happy again and we were getting back to work again.

A model was killed and we were getting mad. It was a Victoria Secret model and she was on the runway last month. She was on vacation here to get away from the media. She was in the right place to get away from the media because the media didn't exist down here. They didn't follow her down here and it was nice and quiet down here. There was stab wounds all over her body suggesting rage. There was a suggestion of vanity issues of the serial killer being jealous of the Victoria Secret model but it was dismissed. There were a few theories out there and they were ridiculous but kept in mind. We had a few things that we had to keep in mind to have a few steps in front of the serial killer. We were thinking the serial killer was trying to kill a variety of different people to throw off the investigators but that was only a theory. I felt like I was six feet from the ledge ready to jump. It was like I was ready to jump and I wanted to stop taking my pills. When I was ready to jump it was like no one wanted to save me. I was scared to jump but it was like I was ready at the same time. I was harmless to everyone and I kept to myself at work. I didn't really talk to anyone at work and it was like they didn't really want to talk to me. I wanted nothing to do with them and they wanted nothing to do with me. They were just keeping to themselves, catching other serial killers and taking bad people off the streets. I was looking for a serial killer I couldn't catch and I was just going to give up soon. There was no way this serial killer was going to get away with these killings much longer. The time was now to catch her and the time for killing for her to keep killing. She was killing so many people and she was a pro killing every day. There was a variety of people she was killing. She was killing a lot of good people including firefighters, cops and daycare providers. It was those kinds of people that deserved to live. She had killed some rapists and pedophiles but not many. There was nothing that made me madder than her killing good people and her killing my family. There was so many people that she had killed that were close to me. It was sad for me and I was going to be the one that was going to suffer for it. My family was suffering more than I was because they had to think about it more. They weren't the ones that were thinking that they were the failure for letting him die. They were feeling that I could have done more to protect him. It was like I wasn't there for him and I was the one that got him killed.

I had asked him to come here to help investigate this case with me. There was no reason why I should have asked him to come investigate this case with me. I had good intentions but if I would have known it would have gotten him killed I would have never asked him to come up from Florida to Minnesota. There was a good thing that I had going now with a good wife but she wasn't turning me on anymore. My love life wasn't what it was five years ago when I got married. I was disappoint in my life and I was looking for something new. I wanted something new. It was like there was nothing new in our love life and there was no spice. There was nothing that I wanted from our love life. I wanted something more from our love life. I wanted something that she wasn't giving me and I didn't know what that was. There was nothing that was going on in our love life that was new. There was nothing that was going on that made things exciting and our sex life was beginning to get dull. I wanted some part of our life to be fifty shades of gray and some parts to be role playing. Then we did role playing and that did nothing. We introduced another girl and that did nothing. I was bored altogether and I was just thinking our love life was ruined. I learned to live with it and get through it and then it got better. There was something that ignited it and I don't know what it was. There was something that made it turn me on. Then we had the best sex of our marriage and that made me happy and we were both happy again. We were both happy and we were having the time of our lives. We were going out to eat at romantic restaurants. It was like we were getting our lives back and we were loving each other. We were like teenagers and we were in stride to have another kid. We held back and we didn't want another kid. We didn't want any more kids and it was like we wanted to have the good life. Then the good life was seeming too good to be true. The good life had to be ruined because we were used to it coming down like a building being demolished. It was like once something was going it had to go bad. There was nothing that seemed right about this and my wife told me not to worry. I was always a constant worrier and it was just like me to be that way. It was how I always was and I didn't know how to be any different. I was always the worrier between the two of us by far. I was always going to be the one that made the big decisions because she didn't want to. We moved into a big house into the country and we loved it. It was a nice house to move into for the family. There was a nice bedroom for us and then the kids got their own room. They loved their room because it was big and we had a nice big yard to play in. We had plenty of things to do to keep us busy. There was nothing I liked to do but keep busy. I was mowing every couple of days and it was nice to keep busy. We had to go to work and get things done. There was nothing like putting in ten hours and then going back home to the family.

There was something about the family that calmed me down. Seeing the family really put a smile on my face. There was nothing that made me happier than family. It made me feel like I was home again. I got to be with the three most important people in the world. There was all this chaos in the world and then it all slowed down when I came home. The chaos began when I drove to work with the busy roads. All the traffic to work with a car crash that slowed things up.

Someone had died in the car crash and it was a big mess. It was the twenty cent killer and it was rare she kill with a car accident. It had happened before but with my sister and that was the only time. This was rare like I said and it was like she was changing her killing style yet again. There was nothing like investigating a kill on your way to work and yet it was the same serial killer you were investigating. It was just bad luck. It was my luck that there were no clues like usual. It was like there was nothing but brakes that were cut. That was what we were left with and there were no fingerprints. That was the usual and we had nothing. We knew the serial killer killed people she didn't know. There was nothing that amazed me more than killings that made her change her killing style.

The next kill was a victim where she snapped their neck and that was a new killing style as well. That was the first time she had snapped someone's neck. There were handprints and that didn't help much and we had nothing else. We were going nowhere with these cases and we had nothing once again. There was a car spotted at the scene and it was a dodge charger two thousand twelve. It was a blue color and that was very helpful possibly stolen. It was dumped a few miles from the crime scene and it had no fingerprints on the steering wheel. There was a bus stop nearby so the killer probably took the bus where she needed to go. That was convenient for her and that was what we had to go on. There wasn't much that we had to go on because there wasn't much that we had for evidence. There was nothing that the serial killer was leaving behind and we had to catch this serial killer before the people started killing each other. It was going to happen and it was going to happen soon. It was going to be where people were going to riot and break into stores. They were going to steal stuff like guns and ammo to feel safe and that was going to be bad. There were going to be break- ins to houses and there were going to be people that were going to steal from other people. It was going to get bad. There was going to be fear in the streets. There was going to be murders and there was going to be crimes like you wouldn't believe. There was going to be anarchy and there was going to be more crime that the police could handle. It was going to get bad and all the people were going to be fearing for their lives. I was fearful that I was going to be pulled off this case soon if I didn't find this serial killer. They would have to find new people and they would have to keep doing the same thing.

There was another kill and it was a model that was blonde. She was on the beach with her face in the water. It was a tragedy for her parents and we had to break the news to them. We couldn't find her fingers and that was the worst part. They weren't kept as trophies by the serial killer I wouldn't think but I wouldn't know for sure. Her teeth were missing too so it was hard to identify her. Someone from the crowd recognized her and that's how we could tell. We told her parents they could bury her after we looked her over for any clues. We didn't find any and that was a shame so we released her to the family. There was no evidence at the crime scene and no blood with the multiple stab wounds to her body. There was a chance that she was killed in a secluded area where no one could ever expect to see them. It was likely that she screamed for help but no one could hear her and that was only a theory. I was thinking that but I didn't say anything. It was only a theory that I kept it to myself. She put up a fight with the front of her hands taking some of the knife wounds. She was a brave girl knowing she was going to die. She was going to die and she put up a good fight. She was about thirty and modeling for multiple magazines. She was a good looking girl and she was in demand. She was going to retire in three years with all the money she had made. She was rich and she could retire so she could live in a modest apartment her family said. I was just glad she lived the full life she did and so was her family. They were proud of what she had done and the lifestyle she had lived. They celebrated her life and had a great turnout for her funeral. They had a lot of food that was eaten and they went home after four hours after the wake. It was a good funeral service. There was a good time at the bars after the funeral with mourning drinks and going home in a cab. Then there was a lot of crying and talking about good times that they had with their daughter. They loved her and they couldn't imagine she was gone. I was waiting for my useless life to end because I was tired of living. I was waiting for the serial killer to end my life so that I could die a hero. The hero was going to die and it was how the story always ended. I read the story of Alex Spencer and his wife Kailee and it was a good story that peaked my interests. It was a story I fell in love with. It was a story that was written by them and it was a story that was told with a lot of action and passion. I had to believe most of it to be true and I was all for it. They wrote it and lived it while working for the devil. Most of it was in the apocalypse. It was a story that was relatable because it was a story where they had to work for their lives knowing nothing more than being poor. They must have known wrong but not caring, not being able to get out or not having a choice. Most of the people that you would have met would have said let's work as a cop or doctor not the devil for ten thousand dollars even if the money is insurmountable. There was a few stories that were in the apocalypse. They were stories that made their ways to the readers and bookstores and they were bestsellers after they were in hell. It would have been a good amount of money for them selling three hundred thousand copies. I figured even if they would have sold one copy the cops would have looked at them and blushed. They would have said look at how many people you killed and got away with it. Now it was time to investigate the next kill and that kill was an auditor. He was killed by being set on fire. That was a surprise and it was going to be hard to know what he looked like. He wasn't going to have an open casket funeral and he was going to be identified by his dental impressions. The family was going to be contacted on what they wanted done with him. It was going to be their decision and I was guessing they were going to cremate him. It was going to be a decision because he was already burnt up. The next kill was someone that did taxes for families out of his home. It was nice of him and now they had to find someone else to do their taxes.

It was going to be hard on them to find someone to do their taxes now because they had been going to him for fifteen years. It was going to be something different for them next year. It was up to 12500 kills and there were going to be a lot of people without families. They were all going through a rough time and I didn't know what to tell them all. Now it was going to be a lot for them to take. There was going to be some people that were going to say that I wasn't doing my job and that wasn't true but it looked that way. There was a time where I was the best at putting serial killers away. Now I was chasing a serial killer that was smarter than me. There was no way that I was thinking I was going to catch this serial killer unless she wanted she wanted me to. I was way out of my league. There was nothing I could do to speed up the process of catching her. She was wearing different perfumes at the crime scenes and it was like she was changing that part of her routine too. There was nothing about that part that was making sense either. I was writing a book about this because I wanted this to be documented. I wanted these family members to know that their kids mattered. I was working on the book and I already had two hundred pages. It was going to sell a few copies and it was going to be a long book. It was going to reveal the serial killer and it was going to tell of my work and sweat that I put into catching this serial killer. The perfume that lead us to knowing that the serial killer was a woman. It was a big break in the case once we knew that because we could release that to the papers. It would alert the families that we had something. That would have the families be on the lookout for suspicious woman lurking around their houses. That would make them be on the lookout and call into the police station. I was going to get a lead. The other people in the office were getting the easy cases and I was getting jealous. I wanted those cases so I could get the easy busts. They were going to get the criminals off the streets and I was going to get my serial killer.

Now it was time to investigate a hit and run. It was the serial killer and it was also a knife to the eye. She had made sure she was dead. It was a brutal murder with four gunshots to the head. It was too much overkill. It was a sign that it was over the edge and there was rage yet again. There was a rage factor that wasn't there before. There was a case that wasn't good enough for an average gunshot to the head. Now it was another kill in the books for the serial killer. It was an oxford student that was visiting her parents and she was killed in her car. When she was hit in a car to car collision she went off the road. She was shot in the head four times and she was just twenty years old going to graduate in a year. She was a girl that had her whole life ahead of her. She was going to graduate a year early from college and she was taking a lot of classes. She was getting A's and it took dedication to keep up those grades. It was that kind of dedication that kept up those grades and those grades didn't come easy. Those grades were from long nights, hard work and sweat. There was nothing that was wrong with taking that many classes and doing that well. There was another murder but it was on campus. It was a quiet day and no one saw anything. No one else was on that floor and it was the perfect time to kill that student. With no one around it was the perfect crime and she exited the right door so one saw her leave. I was surprised at this and everyone was there when we sealed off the crime scene. Anyone could be there as long as they stayed behind the yellow tape. It was a tragedy for everyone that seen her dead. There was nothing that she did that to piss people off. She had a lot of friends and she was liked by everyone that wasn't a friend. She was also a good tutor to a lot of students. She knew a lot about math and she was a genius in science. It was a good thing she was a tutor because she was one of the best tutors the school had. She was a good athlete too. She was in track, lacrosse and soccer and juggling a lot of things at once. She had a busy work schedule and it wasn't easy having her life. Now that she was dead she had a lot of kids that mourned her. A lot of people remembered her at school. They prayed for her at school and they had a memorial for her at school. They remembered her like they were supposed to. They were remembering her like she was a family member that had passed and that was nice of them. She was like family to them and that was like they had lost a sister. She was in a sorority for two years that she loved. It was a good thing for her because she was shy when she joined. It made her outgoing and it made it so she could make friends. There was nothing she did that made her a bad egg. She was a girl that got straight A's and it was impressing her parents. If you were smart enough to get into Oxford then it was great for a resume and a job. It was far away and expensive but it was worth it. It was a scholarship and she had earned it. She was dedicated to earning it and saying that she deserved it. She proved that she deserved it. This was a girl that made no mistakes in school and had many friends and no enemies. She got killed in the prime of her life and it was tragic.

There was another kill in an alley and it was a stab wound to the chest with a lot of blood. There were shoe impressions and it was a clue we needed. It looked like a size nine shoe and it was a clue that we could use although there were many people that used a sixe nine shoe. It looked like Asics shoes. According to our experts it was a very old shoe and no one hardly wore that type of shoe anymore. That was a good clue and now we had to find out if there were any witnesses. There wasn't and that was just our luck. I drank a few Bud Light Platinums and it was something to get my mind off the case. My mind wasn't in these cases because I wasn't catching this serial killer so what was the point? I wasn't going to catch this serial killer anytime soon and all I needed was that one clue that was going to going to lead me to the serial killer. I was so close that I could taste it in the back of my throat. I needed this so I could retire as a cop and work back at Wal-Mart. I wasn't getting any younger and I was aging like expired milk and that was the cold hard truth. There was nothing I could do but wait for a witness to identify the serial killer. I needed to get a sketch and that wasn't going to happen anytime soon. I needed a make on the stolen car that wasn't going to be abandoned. That was going to the break in the case that we needed. There was going to be a break in the case sooner or later. I was going to work and making no progress. I was getting sick of everything. All the kills and no progress in the cases not knowing who the serial killer was and all the good people dying. There needed to be more serial killers, rapists and pedophiles killed by this serial killer. There wasn't enough of that and I wanted more of that to keep me going. If there was more of that I would be happier as crazy as that sounded. There was a crazy sickness to that but I didn't care because there was nothing that I had to explain to people. The kills were piling up and the killer's method of killing was changing.

The next kill was a snapped neck and that wasn't any different. There was nothing that was new about this kill because the serial killer had killed like this before. It was like it was something that was going to be a regular thing for the serial killer. It was a regular killer because the serial killer killed the next four victims by snapping their necks. The next eight victims were beaten to death. We had to look at this like a pattern and routine. There was nothing that was making sense about these killings.

She had never killed these victims with the same method of killing this many times in a row. There was nothing that made sense when it came to this.

It was different and the next kill was a housewife and her kids were teenagers. They were all killed taking naps and it was all stab wounds. They were all stabbed seventeen times and there was blood on the ceiling and walls. The beds and had blood and the husband walked in and found the murders and called the police. The police arrived in ten minutes. We were all there and I took over the crime scene and found no evidence like usual. There was something that was different. The shoe impressions were size ten and that was what threw us off. It wasn't a different killer and it was weird. I knew I was going to deal with something that was going to be different. They were Adidas shoes according to our expert. I was going to think about this for a long time. This was something that was weird because usually there was blood left behind if there was a stabbing. I figured she climbed on the bed because the mom was in the middle of the bed and she got blood on her shoes. It looked like a careless kill and I didn't understand it. I wasn't impressed with this crime like the other crimes. There was nothing that was going on with this crime because it wasn't organized. I was concerned for the serial killer that she was going to get caught soon. There was evidence against her in a few crimes and I was going to catch her with this evidence. This was going to seal the case. This case was going to be the evidence that was going to catch her. It was going to be presented in court. There was going to be no other evidence. With the other evidence we could tie her to the crimes.

There was a stripper killed and she was in an alley and she was a blonde. She was about thirty three and skinny as a twig. She had a lot of family members that cared about her. She had five brothers and sisters and they all wondered where she was. They hadn't seen her in a couple days and now they knew. Their worst fears were confirmed and they knew she was dead. When I came to their door they knew why I was there. They were crying when I told them it was a serial killer we were hunting. It was someone we were going to catch soon. We were going to do everything we could to bring her to justice. We wanted her dead and it was a strong wish. It was a something that I wasn't going promise. Everyone wanted her dead and it was a long line to wait for. Everyone that had lost a loved one to the serial killer and wanted her dead. There was nothing I wanted more than her head on a silver platter but I had to serve justice not vengeance. There was a certain code we had to live by. We only took a life by self-defense and that was still considered murder. That was something you had to live with. It was something that the families of the people you had killed will hate you for the rest of your life. They took all of those moments for granted. It was those moments that you were supposed to cherish and love. When you say the wrong words and die you wish you could take them back knowing you can't. Then they die that's when you regret fighting. I was watching a movie with Sarah and the kids and it was close to seven. Now I wanted to go to bed when the doorbell rang. It was our friends and we talked for a couple hours. They had told us their son died a couple of years ago from a house fire and it sounded like the serial killer. They werent home and it was arson. I didn't like it but it was something that she could have left behind. We had a couple of hours and then we went to their place and we continued drinking and it was a fun time. We were having a fun time when I got a call.

Then there was an escaped convict that got killed. It was the serial killer and he was back to killing the usual bad guys. He had been dead for four hours and it was good for us because the cops didn't have to look for him. The cops found him with full rigamortis set in. They were looking for him and finally found him. Hikers found him in the woods and it was lucky for the cops. It was good because he could have been in Mexico. He didn't end up taking a car. It was good he didn't think of taking a car because he would have gone anywhere he wanted. The serial killer did a favor for us because he was a good citizen that day. The next kill was a rapist and he was a danger to society. He would have killed and raped again. It would have been a disaster. There would have been a lot of victims scared for their lives locking their doors wondering if they would be safe.

There was another kill and it was a cheerleader. It was very hard to identify her without a head or fingers. There was nothing we could do but ask the school if they were missing a cheerleader. They said her name was Amber Mchutchins and she was getting a B average. It was a good grade point average and everyone thought she was a nice girl. A lot of people liked her and her personality. Her boyfriend was really upset and we contacted her parents and they cremated her. They had a funeral and it was a small get together for the family. They all said a few words and it was a good get together. There was nothing that the students did that was going to bring their beloved student back. They held a memorial service for Amber and they remembered their favorite student and classmate. There was nothing they wanted more than to have her back and to talk to her for one more day. They wanted a couple more minutes to say goodbye and say that they loved her. They wanted to say how great she was and to make her feel wanted. There was nothing that was there next year because she would have been graduated. There was another kill and it was a lacrosse player and he was the top scorer on his team. He was at our college and he was a pretty good player. He was going to be missed by his fellow teammates. He was a key part in their success and without them they couldn't win. They weren't going to have a winning season next season and they were going to have to find another great player to replace him. He was a great player and the team took a moment of silence to remember him before their next game. It was nice of them to do that. I was miserable with my family and the family life wasn't for me anymore. I wanted out of this life because I was bored. Life wasn't worth living. I was sick of my wife and I was sick of her working late. My kids were a bore and I was thinking of eating a bullet. I wanted to end my life. I didn't want to do it but I was strongly considering it. My kids were always needing attention and they were always complaining they were bored. They always wanted me to buy them things. Money was the ultimate evil and it drove this world. It was all depressing and I hated it. I wanted to end it all. It was all going to end hopefully and it was going to end soon. It was all just a bore and it was all the same. Someone was always getting murdered and I was waking up, running the kids off to school investigating a murder and not knowing who did it. That was all the same as long as the killer didn't come after my wife or my kids I was good. I was just happy my wife or kids weren't dead yet. There was a certain quickness to the kills. The killer was in and out quick and left within a short time span. It gave us less time to catch up to her. That was the hard part, catching up to all her kills and investigating each and every kill thoroughly. There was nothing I wanted more than to connect her to all these crimes. We needed a fingerprint to do that or her blood at the crime scene. Some clue like that to do something so that we could do something big. Take the horse by the reigns and lead it to the water. There was nothing we were doing right to catch this serial killer. There was going to be a break in the case soon, I could feel it. Now there was another kill.

It was a volleyball player and she was about fourteen years old. She was a redhead and she was missing her fingers and all her teeth. It was going to be easy to identify her. Her teammates knew who she was and they told us she was Mckayla James. She was loved by all her volleyball players but they didn't love her. It was a loss to all of them. She was an all around player and her parents were heartbroken. They were just wondering how it could have happened to them. It was every family that thought that. There was something that was murky in the waters. There was something that didn't feel right because all of this was starting to feel weird. The killer was all of a sudden starting to kill all these teens. She was killing so many in a row. She hadn't done this before. This was not like her.

She killed an elderly couple and both had served in the military a long time ago. It was something that they both had in common. They married in the military from what their kids had told us. They were in love from the first time they met each other.

They never took their eyes off each other like star crossed lovers. There was nothing that separated them, not even death. Now they were in a better place. God took them because it was simply their time. They had a job to do for God. They had helped out at church for many years and now they were going to help out God in a different way. There was nothing that was going to happen that wasn't going to get them into heaven. There was going to be a good life for them in heaven. They were going to be happy in life after death. There was nothing that love couldn't conquer. There was a lot that they did for themselves. They liked going out for picnics with their children and going to action movies. It was good for them to get out. I was sleeping with the girl that I originally went out with when I was cheating on my wife. My wife didn't know and the husband didn't know either. There was a secrecy that was kind of naughty dangerous and exciting. I was like doctor danger and I was thrilled at this. I was excited to be cheating. There was a temptation in this and I wanted to leave my wife for this girl. It was a certain danger that made it exciting. It made me feel free from my marriage and it made me feel so alive. Who the hell did I think I was to think I could cheat and get away with it? I felt like a cheating piece of crap. My luck was going to run out and my wife was going to find out and kick my ass. She was going to throw me out of the house or throw me on the couch. She was going to make me sleep there for a while and not talk to me. She would give me the silent treatment for a few weeks and give me shitty food for as long as she wanted. I was wanting to cheat for as long as it took to get my life back together so I could have a happy life again. My wife patched things up again and then we started having sex again. We were going to movies and going to work like regular people. Then we were going to picnics, camping, swimming and things like that. We were having fun but we weren't going on vacation like I wanted. There were things that I wanted to do that I couldn't do because I had my job. That made me mad because there were people that I worked with that could take trips. They were happy with that and I wanted to be happy like they were. They were happy taking trips while I was pissed taking camping trips and going on picnics and going to movies. I was getting mediocre paychecks and it was making me mad. There was nothing that was making me happy and it was all one big joke. It was like looking in the mirror and having your reflection laugh at you. It was pathetic being me and I was just a joke. I wanted to catch the serial killer I was after so I could sleep at night without tossing and turning. My wife wanted me to sleep at night too but she couldn't comfort me. She was doing everything she could to comfort me but nothing was helping. I was helping on the case and nothing was sticking. It was like the serial killer was taunting us with every kill. It was like the killer was saying Hey come look at who I killed, investigate it and see if you can catch me. See if you can keep up while I kill the next victim. It was a taunting technique that I knew all too well and it was like she did this with every kill. There was nothing to do but ask what I should do with every case. The person to ask was my psychiatrist and she had no answers. There were no answers and no one was going to have anything to do with me. Only the serial killer was going to have the answers and the answers were going to be so clear like the ocean water. It was going to be like the answers flooding in like the knowledge you so desperately crave. There was nothing I needed more than those answers. Those answers were going to come when the serial killer was caught. When she was caught the answers were going to be clear. My sacrifice was putting all this work into these cases and it was going to pay off at one point. It was all this sacrifice that was going to show in the end. They were all going to appreciate it. All the cops, all the families and the serial killer because the serial killer liked me. The killer was going to lead me to her when she was ready. She was going to leave a clue because she was cocky and desperate to put on a show for everyone to see. She was going to lead me to her and that was what she said in one of her letters and I believed her. The next kill was a hobo and he was beaten to death with a pot and that was ironic. It was ironic because he had just eaten at a soup kitchen. It was just something that I found ironic. No one found ironic because I didn't bring it up. There was nothing that I wanted from these cases. I wanted this serial killer caught but I didn't care if these cases were solved because he wasn't going to be tried for these cases. These cases had no evidence and he wouldn't be tried. There wasn't anything we could do about it. Without any evidence we couldn't try him. There was nothing that was admissible in court so why would we bring it to court? Now the next case was weird. There was a museum owner that was stabbed with a dinosaur bone. It was weird to me and he was worth fifty million dollars. That was worth a little bit of money. Now they were going to have to find a new owner. There was nothing that was normal about this case. There was something that was odd about this case. This killer hadn't killed too many museum owners. How did she know he was the museum owner? Maybe it was a lucky guess but lucky wasn't even close to how she knew if he was the museum owner or not.

The next kill was a painter and he was stabbed with his own sharpened paintbrush. It was kind of ironic. She was a struggling artist that painted beautiful drawings. She had painted a bird flying over glaciers. She had painted a dog running through tall grass and a dog on a porch with his owner in a rocking chair. They were beautiful paintings and she was getting decent amounts for her paintings. It was enough to get by but she needed more to pay her bills. She had to pay more bills so she had a second job. That was stressful enough and she was working odd hours. She was working fourteen hours and weekends and it was taking its toll. It was like there was no end. There was no end and there was a painting career to think of. Wal- Mart wasn't her dream job. Painting was her passion and she didn't like her boss. She hated the hours and she liked the free flowing of paint. The colors and the calmness of the brush strokes was what made her happy. But now that she was dead so she couldn't paint the imagination in her mind. There were going to be a lot of painters that she inspired with her paintings even if she didn't think so. She was a good painter and her paintings were handed to her parents. It was a nice gesture and it was good for them to do that. They were copies but it was a good gesture like I said. It was like they had paintings of hers that lived on through her. There was a kindness to her paintings and there was a movement as well. It was so free flowing that it captured your attention and it was hard to look away. There was nothing that was bad about any of these paintings. I loved these paintings so much I bought these paintings at the stores when I saw them. They were masterpieces when I saw them. They were just amazing and I fell in love with them and I had to have them. There was a certain free flowing art to them when I saw them. When the artist got stabbed there was a great talent that was taken from this world. The world was missing the talent that it couldn't get back. The parents were heartbroken and it was like losing the life that was like your dog to a very little child. It was like the child's very best friend and that was what it was like for this family. They had lost their best friend, their only child and their baby girl to them. She was always going to be their baby girl and it was like a piece of them was lost. They were supposed to die before her and it was a tragedy that she was buried with twenty roses on top of her casket. She was remembered with dignity and praise. She had great appreciation and accomplishment. It was a lot to take in and they buried her on a Friday. She was buried on a rainy day and it was a killing day for us.

It was an electrician and a firefighter electrocuted and burned alive. One was forty three and one was thirty five and they were both great men. They were both good family members and they were both married with three children. It was a coincidence and they were both married to beautiful woman. It was going to be hard raising a family of three and finding a job for a housewife. It was going to be hard for a single mother to pay for daycare. There was going to be a lot of money involved in that and I wouldn't want to front the bill for that. There was going to be a big bill for daycare and it was going to be two hundred some bucks a week or more. It was going to be spendy and I didn't know how she was going to afford it. I was going to go to work, forget about it and move onto the next case. The next case was a knife to the heart. From the looks of it and how deep it was it looked like the serial killer had thrown it with force. It was thrown pretty hard and from a pretty fair distance away. I'd say she threw it from ten feet away. There was another kill that was really weird and that was a baby. I didn't understand that because out of all the kills you had to kill a baby? Come on out of all the kills it had to be a baby? It was heartless and only a monster would do this. A monster committed this murder and devil was wearing this mask. it was clear that we were dealing with someone without a soul. We were going to have to take care of this monster before she killed another baby because it was going to happen.

The next set of kills was just as bad because it was an orphanage. It was a bad mixture of chemistry and disaster. It was an explosive mixture of chaos when they were put together. It was like chaos was her middle name if anyone knew her middle name. No one was going to know her by any other name besides the monster known as chaos. The monster that created chaos was the way she operated. There was all this death and destruction. Then there was all this murder and it never stopped. It all seemed like a dream that you couldn't wake up from. It all seemed more like a nightmare that was getting worse after every kill. No one knew what I was going through. I was just going through a lot now and it was just like I was torn between catching a serial killer and trying to balance my family life. I was just failing in every aspect of my life and times were trying. People were trying to help but I wouldn't let them. I was going on a lot of walks but it didn't seem to help. I was trying to listen to music to drown out the world. It was helping sometimes but other times it was like the world was taking over. The world was taking over and I was taking the world on like I used to. I wasn't confident in myself anymore. It was like I was getting used to the world screwing me over. The world was screwing me over and spitting me out. I was getting in front of the dragon and the dragon was breathing fire on me. The bull was running straight at me and I was the red cape. I was the one that was getting run over by the car and being left in the ditch. It was like I was numb to the pain. The pain felt good and without the pain I was feeling nothing. Without the pain I couldn't feel alive. There was nothing to feel without the pain and I wasn't tapping out until my arm popped out of socket. I was too hard on myself and I was in fear of losing myself. I was in fear of losing who I was as a person. I was a terrible husband for cheating and I was slacking off. I was cheating on and my wife and she didn't know it. I was bored with my life and I had no drive in the car on the road to life. There were twists and turns on the road but the power steering was going out. There was nothing I could do but pay the money for the power steering with the money I didn't have hypothetically of course. There was nothing that made me happy and I wondered if I was depressed or just going through a rut. Maybe it was a midlife crisis. My midlife crisis had started up again and I think it had originally started a couple of weeks ago. There was nothing I could do about my midlife crisis and my life was going down the shitter. It was just like I had nothing to live for. There was something that made me go nuts and it was the serial killer getting in my head. There was nothing to do but eat a bullet or get through it with my wife and hope that it gets better. Everything was going to get better but it was the question of when. I thought that we were going to catch the serial killer soon but then another year passed. It was just hurting me that the serial killer was taunting me every day and that we weren't catching her. She was killing hookers a lot. She had a special hatred for hookers and porn stars. There was nothing worse than hookers and porn stars for her. It was getting to her and that was what we knew. That was the worst kind of people for her because she was stabbing them thirty times. That was a certain kind of rage. It was a special kind of rage that she was getting out. She was taking out her rage by stabbing them and that was a special kind of hatred. She was mad at every single one of them and it was just scratching the surface. We didn't know why she was mad at them. We were trying to find out why she had a rage towards these hookers and porn stars. Maybe it was their professions and their looks. We didn't know but it didn't matter. All that mattered was catching this monster. This monster had a mask that we had to reveal. We had to take off the mask and reveal the monster. It was the monster that was going to eat us alive if we weren't careful. If we weren't alive it was going to consume us and our souls. We were going to be the ones who were going to be the monsters if we didn't catch this serial killer soon. Someday I was going to look back on this and look at all the hard work I put into this and finally appreciate it.

There was a body in the alley and her head was chopped off along with her fingers. There was a lot of blood at the crime scene but that was the usual. Her hands were missing along with her feet and it was a grisly murder. It was going to be another long case. We were going to solve this but there was going to be no end to these crimes. This was the worst serial killer in history. There was no end to her killing spree and it was going to be a long case load. It was a lot of families calling in wondering if they could sleep at night. They were wondering if we had found their family member's killer. No we hadn't and it was going to be a long time before we did. There was a madness to these crimes and the madness was only beginning. The madness was a sickness fed for a desire to kill. The desire for her to kill was strong. It was like it was something that was so strong it was hard for her to control. She had to kill every day to control her appetite.

There was a bomb that went off next to us. All the cop cars and firetrucks were lined up for miles waiting for action. The bomb squad could do nothing because the bomb already went off. It was like no one wanted to help us out. It was just great I said sarcastically. It was just our luck. No one felt like they wanted to be in the helping mood. I recorded the new episode of suits and went to bed hoping the next day would be better. I went to bed early anticipating that something was going to happen the next day. It didn't so I was excited. There was a kill that was so badass that I couldn't figure out how she pulled off this kill. It was a CIA agent and it was such a difficult kill. I couldn't wrap my head around such difficulty. He had the best security system in the world with best security team. I knew he had around the clock team and security system that was up to date so it was really weird that someone got in his house. She must have picked off all the security agents in one go and made it look like a kindergarten game. He killed the CIA agent in a couple of swift seconds before the police caught wind of her. She was fast and took care of business. She was good and I gave her props for taking care of business so quickly. I envied her but I wasn't going to give her props for showing all of her poker chips all at once. You cant do that if you want to win a poker game. She was the best for a reason.

The next kill was a good kill because she took on a martial arts instructor that knew karate and kick boxing. He was good and she was better. She was the best and he was beaten to death. The fight had taken place in his house and there were a lot of things that were broken. I imagined it was a good fight. There were so many holes in the wall and that meant there were a few misses. there were a lot of bruised body parts a lot of broken bones. That meant this was an experienced serial killer and she was trained in a very particular set of fighting styles. It was like she knew how to kick box and martial arts. She had to in order to beat the martial artist instructor who also knew kickboxing and karate. It was like she knew everything about him and how to beat him. She was a miracle fighter and I was impressed. It was the hardest fight she had to overcome. It was like she was a martial arts instructor herself but there were only a few martial artist instructors in town. That narrowed it down to a few people. If she kept killing them that meant she was going to reveal herself. The next kill was over the top and I was surprised because he was better than any fighter that I had ever seen. I didn't hardly want to say who he was but I was going to anyway.

He was a shaolin monk and he had come down from far away down from the mountains. He was from the highest mountains and he was from one of the coldest mountains. He had moved here to the simple life for a while to train people on how to fight. He was one of the best fighters in the world because no one could fight like him. He was dead from the serial killer beating him to death. His martial arts were like no other. He must have trained her at a young age and she must have mastered the art. She must have trained with him at a younger age and mastered the art and come back to kill him. He was dead and she was serious about killing the best fighters in the world. It was clear she wasn't messing around. It was going to be a long road to catching this serial killer. The road was going to be rocky and if the path was uncertain then we had to be certain of what we knew. There was nothing we knew besides the serial killer was a girl and she changed shoes and shoe sizes to throw us off. It was like she liked dicking us around and playing with us like a cat. A cat likes playing with a ball of yarn and a mouse likes outsmarting a cat. It was like if I closed my eyes it would all go away but I knew it wasn't true. I wanted it to be true because this case had dragged on for twenty six years and I was fifty six. It was a ripe old age and I was tired and old. I didn't want to do this anymore. My wife was fifty one and she was tired of me coming home miserable because I couldn't catch this serial killer. All the while I was running on fumes staying up all night tossing and turning thinking about it. This was getting to me and I was growing into something that was different compared to what I used to be. There was nothing that was good about me anymore. I was thinking like the serial killer and it was like I was fusing in the mind of the serial killer. I was getting home later investigating more crimes than usual and it was taking its toll. It was like there was something holding me back from solving this case and I didn't know what it was. It was damaging to my career. It was making it look like I was a bad cop. It made it look like I was the cop that couldn't catch a serial killer after so many years. There was nothing I wanted more than to go home at a decent hour and spend more time with my kids and watch them grow up. It was like they were growing up without a father and a mother. There was an empty space in their lives and they were spending more time at the daycare than at home. There was nothing we could do about that because we had we had to work these hours to put food on the table. We were busting our butts every day to put criminals behind bars without any appreciation. I was still working other cases and taking criminals off the streets but most of my time was dedicated to looking for the serial killer. There was nothing we had for evidence besides perfume and a footprint. It was nothing to go on and it was frustrating. It was nothing that made us happy. There was nothing made us get any closer to the serial killer. There were things we needed to know about the serial killer in order to catch her and we didn't have that information. We needed a sketch and we didn't have that. We also had no witnesses that saw her and no license plate information. We didn't have any information leading to the serial killer. She was going to continue with her killing spree that was going to go on for another couple of months or years. We didn't know how many more people she was going to kill but we hoped it wasn't going to be another thousand or more. There was already seventeen thousand dead and that was the most on record. There was nothing that made me madder than seventeen thousand people dead. She was killing almost every day and we were barely keeping up. There was no sense to her killing all these people and it was senseless crimes. She robbed a couple of banks and killed a couple of tellers. She also killed the manager of the bank. There was nothing that made sense about killing them. It was organized and the witnesses said there were four people. They were all wearing ski masks. It was the serial killer because she had left twenty cents on the desk. It was in and out of the vault in a minute and a half. There was no security and they killed the two bank tellers working so they couldn't set off the silent alarm. There was three hundred and seventy thousand dollars stolen and it was organized. It was like they knew who to kill and they knew which bank to rob. It was all the money they could carry. They had five big duffel bags and it was good for them that they didn't get caught. It was the first bank robbery and they did it again at a different bank. This time getting four hundred thousand and it was organized. They killed all the bank tellers and the manager so he couldn't set the silent alarm in his office. They knew what they were doing. The cops didn't get there in time and it was in and out after that. It was a stolen car and it was ditched and they walked somewhere that the cops couldn't track them. They went somewhere that the cops couldn't find them. They robbed one more bank and split the money before parting ways. There was nothing that was wrong with retiring from robbing banks but they never spent money on extravagant things. There was nothing that was going to make the news that was interesting. They had all the murders on the news which was the only reason I watched the news. There was nothing interesting on the news besides the bank robberies so I watched sports center. I bought a Richard Sherman jersey and I walked to the mall and bought a Vikings hat. I bought some pants with a cool design on the pocket. There was nothing that made sense to me about these killings. There was so many killings that we weren't going to solve. It was impossible to stop the families from walking into the station. They were demanding answers and asking what we were doing to solve their family's cases. We were doing nothing because we had nothing. We were telling them we were doing everything we could like usual. We had no leads and we were depending on the public for help. They weren't helping us like we had hoped. They weren't surviving the attacks because all these family members were dying. We couldn't figure out the next victim or how she was choosing her victims.

The next kill she chose was an institutionalized patient. She got a keycard from somebody got into the facility killed him and left. No one saw her and she left without leaving a fingerprint. She was caught on camera but she had her head down the whole time and it was a good technique. There was nothing made sense to me about this because it didn't seem like she had been in this facility before. It didn't seem like she knew where the cameras were so how did she know when to keep her head down? It didn't make sense to me but it was smart on her part and she walked into the facility like she had been there before. I knew she couldn't have been there if she had to pick the lock of the house, kill someone and take their I.D. It was a kill that was very difficult to take because one of my cousins was in a psych ward and he was still taking pills. It was still damaging his mind and he would never be the same. He didn't want to take pills and he was fifteen at the time. Now he is eighteen and refused to take his pills while in the psych ward even though he needed the pills. He didn't think he needed the pills but he did. He was weaned off them and he finally didn't need them. He was on something else that he did want to take. He was living on his own and it was nice for him.

The next kill was a private investigator. He was

making seventy thousand dollars a year. He was a private investigator and it was a dangerous job for him. He was in shootouts a lot and he was going to get himself in trouble. He was taking dangerous jobs for the thrill and it was something that he liked. He was now doing easier jobs that didn't shooting and it involved cheating spouses and taking pictures of them. It wasn't glamourous but it was good money. It was seven hundred bucks per job. It was a lot of money for one job and he got good results. Most of them were cheating but some of them weren't. If they weren't he gave them their money back and that was nice of him. He was a nice guy like that and he knew how to treat his client's right. There was a lot of clients that he had because he was good at his job. His job was to make money and he made a lot of money. The next kill was a stockbroker and he was taking everyone's money. He was a crook like every one of them and it was a good thing that she killed her. She was a crook that needed to die whether she got killed by the serial killer or someone else. There was a satisfaction that I got when this stockbroker died as selfish as that sounded. I was still working thirteen hours instead of fourteen hours and it was taking a toll on my family. My wife was still staying late at work too. She was staying at work later than me and that was a problem. She was staying at work all hours of the night. I thought we would have similar work schedules and that wasn't the case. She looked me in the face and said she wasn't cheating and I believed her. I had no reason not to believe her. There was a side to her that I saw that no one else did. I was beginning to think she had a whole other life outside of the house. She was staying out late and I didn't know if it was work or something else. I wanted to know where she was going at night if she wasn't working. There was nothing I wanted to know more than what she was doing at work because it was different than what I was doing at work. I think it was working sex crimes. There was nothing worse than working sex crimes because you get attached to the victims. You feel sorry for them and you want to hit the bad guys every chance you get. There was nothing worse than a rapist and a pedophile in my book and they were going to get it in jail. She loved working sex crimes because she could put the bad guys behind bars. They would go to jail for up to ten years and that was good enough for her.

There was a rapist that had escaped from jail and he was on the run for four days. He turned up dead and it was the serial killer. He was in the woods and he was facedown. He had twenty cents on his neck and it was a gunshot to the back of the head. There was a blood pool on the ground and it was a mess. It was obvious he had been brought here and killed by the serial killer. I didn't know how she had found him and no one else did either. None of us knew anything but there were tire tracks and they weren't fresh. We put plaster over the tracks and we knew it was the car that the serial killer was driving. It was the only tire tracks and it was the clue we needed. It was going to be the clue that was going to solve the case. There was glass in the victim's leg and it was a clue and we needed that clue too. We were going to solve the case with that clue too and that was going to bring us closer to the serial killer too. We found the car that had the kicked out back window and it had a sweaty fingerprint on the volume knob. It was another good clue. It was going to be the useful break in the case that we would be hoping for. There was good evidence there and it was going to lead us to the serial killer. The serial killer finally made a mistake and it was making her look like an amateur but she wasn't in the system. There was nothing that was making this easy on us. It was making our jobs more difficult. We thought we had good evidence but we had nothing that we could use yet again. There was nothing we could do with this evidence and it was like we were at the end of the rope and at the drawing board back at square one. We were going to use this evidence in some way. Maybe she was convicted of a minor crime and we could search the other data bases. It could be a possibility and we could try it and it was something we were going to do it. She was killing so long that we were willing to try anything and we had seen her kill eighteen thousand people. Everything was coming undone before our eyes and it was becoming clear that we were going to catch her soon. There was a chance that the evidence on the volume button was going to convict her. There was a good lead in this sweaty print here and I was sure we were going to convict her on this and I was going to catch her soon. If she had a criminal record we were going to convict her.

The next kill was a gambler and that was his career and he was very good at it. He would make ten thousand a time and it was amazing. He would get lucky at poker and it was like he would count cards. There were many times he was hitting a twenty one and that was amazing to me. The dealer would get eighteen and seventeen and he would get twenty one. It was great for him and bad for the dealer. It was fun for him and it was something that was going good for him until he died. He got his money stolen by the serial killer and she spent the money on a car that was never found. It was a nice car too and and it was a nice used car. It had one hundred thousand miles on it and it was a convertible. I was amazed and I was getting mad that this serial killer had this much money to spend. She had hundreds of thousands of dollars that she didn't spend. She was somewhere where we couldn't find her. She was hiding it somewhere and we couldn't find it. She was going to spend it at one point or another and it was going to be her downfall.

The next kill was a tourist and she was visiting from Chicago. She was visiting for a week and her car was missing. It turned up in an abandoned building and it was a weird spot to turn up. There was no way the serial killer could get away but she did and it was weird that she kept getting away with murder even though there was a fingerprint that we had. There was nothing that we had and there was nothing we could do to match that fingerprint to. There was nothing that my instincts told me that was saying that I knew who it was. It didn't match anyone in the system so that was a bust and it was going to be a good thing if she revealed herself to us but it wasn't going to happen. She was spreading her peacock feathers again and they were beautiful and she was showing off again. She liked showing off and putting on a show for us. There was always a show put on in our honor. There was always something that she had to prove and we didn't know why. There was always going to be a show put on for us by the serial killer and she was always going to be top dog. The next kill was a victim that had forty seven stab wounds and she was face down in an alley. She was a model and she was a beautiful tall girl. She was about five eight and she was a blonde orphan girl and she was adopted at age five. She had very nice parents and she was taken care of by very wealthy parents and she got whatever she wanted. She was the only child in her family and she was spoiled. She deserved it for not being adopted until she was five. She was the best kid and she was the kid that had a lot of friends. She loved everyone that wasn't her friend and everyone loved her. There was no one that didn't like her and she had no bullies. There were a lot of kids in her school. I would say about seven hundred kids and it was a lot to me. There were two hundred kids graduating in her class alone and that was a lot. That was a big number and she was very smart kid. She was taking hard classes and getting A's and I was impressed. She was going to go to college in a year and she didn't get that chance. She was saving up money and it was going to be a lot for school. There was going to be a lot left over for an apartment. There was going to be some money earned for paying a lot of bills too. She had a pretty nice car and she had a lot of health insurance. She had a boyfriend and she was getting out of the business in a month. She was getting another job and working as a stripper in a nightclub. It was going to pay better money and not be as disease ridden. It was going to secure her boyfriend and her boyfriend liked that better and had suggested that. She was into that and he had found that sexy. He was going to move in with her.

The next kill was a lawyer and his winning percentage was eighty seven percent. That was pretty good in my book and he owned his own firm with three other lawyers. He was the best and his lawyers were pretty good too. They were top of the line and they knew it too. They liked to win and they had clients coming in weekly and they were always keeping busy. They were always going to miss him. They were losing clients because their best lawyer was gone but they were getting a lot of clients because of their reputation. They were getting more clients than usual after a while and it was amazing that they did better without him. It was great that their reputation was better without him. There was a common motto they had we win because you help us win. It was cheesy but it worked and it was getting them clients. It was their motto that got them clients. It was their motto that made them legitimate. If you have a good slogan and catch 22 you will hook at least one person. Now they needed a leader and they found one when they hired someone else. It was someone they hired that got them more clients than they were ever getting before. They were getting five clients a day compared to three. They had five lawyers with a hectic office and they were winning cases left and right. They were all dead by the serial killer and the serial killer must have hated all of them. It was all over for this office and they were forced to close down shop. The people were going to have to find new lawyers to represent them. It was a tragedy for them and it was going to be the worst thing for them because their winning rate was ninety seven percent. They were winning like crazy because they weren't taking a huge percentage like so many others. It was fair to them and it was like they demanded very little for such big settlements. The clients were getting paid thousands and the lawyers weren't getting paid much at all. They were going to be known as the best lawyers in our town and they were going to go down as the best lawyers that ever lived. They would be remembered as the best and it was going to be a big loss. We weren't going to find any better lawyers than that and that was why it was so sad. There was a mistake in the papers because a lawyer had survived and he was on life support. He had pulled through and he practiced in a different town when he pulled through. He was left alone after that and I was glad because a good lawyer like that should be allowed to practice and have a good life after near death. He was shot in the head and it had grazed his head and the serial killer thought she had killed him. He had bled out enough to look like he had died but that was a fool's play and that was why she thought he died. He had stopped breathing for a while and it was scary but he pulled through and now he was in a different town practicing law. There was no reason he should have pulled through and it was a miracle and an act of God. I wasn't staying up until all hours of the night thinking about who the serial killer was as a person or as a deep minded individual. I was thinking about who she was going to kill next or if she was going to kill me. There was mystery to this and it was kind of making me want to get this case wrapped up that much quicker. There was nothing that made me want to think of anything else but who the serial killer was. That was all I was thinking about at night. I was thinking of drinking and doing drugs again but that didn't seem like an option. There was nothing that made me think that I knew this serial killer until I got a letter saying otherwise. The letter said

"You should know who I am by now, I left a sweaty fingerprint behind and I am very close to you. That is all the information you need to know to catch me

I was fascinated by this and I now knew the serial killer was related to me but who did I know that was related to me? I had to keep the letter to myself because there would be speculation around the office and there was no fingerprints on it anyways so there were no clues. It was nothing that I needed to hand into the police because they would just suspect all my family and bring them in for questioning and I didn't need that. They would all be suspects and that was the last thing that I wanted and I wouldn't put them through that so I burned the letter. That was the last thing that was on mind but then again I couldn't stop thinking about it a couple of days later. It was troubling me and I didn't know what to do. It was like I needed a bath to wash off all the guilt and the suspicion from the family. There was going to be paranoia in my mind of who could it be and what was I up against was I safe from my family? It was all unclear and I had to make it all clear. There was going to be some clarity when I caught the serial killer and it was going to be so obvious and I needed this to be solved whether I wanted to work at Wal-Mart or not. Wal-Mart wasn't the ideal job but it was the job I was used to and I liked it better than this cop job I was working. I was staying up late watching forensic files and it was like I was running on fumes and I was just pissed that I wasn't finding the serial killer. She was killing important people like CEOs of companies and it was frustrating because they were really big and successful companies and they needed these people to succeed and we needed these companies in our town. We needed these companies in our town to thrive and she was destroying it all. It was frustrating and I wanted her head on a platter for this. It was all going downhill from here. I was taking more walks to calm my nerves and sometimes it helped and sometimes it made me more mad and anxious. I paced a lot more and it made me more anxious at times and I was thinking of ways I could kill the serial killer. It was cold and demented and I didn't really care at this point. I was getting edgy towards my co-workers and they were getting mad at me and I couldn't help it. I was just high strung and the serial killer was just getting to me. I was cutting myself to feel something and my cuts were turning to scars. I was wearing long shirts and stopped cutting. I started drinking at the bars more often. I went out drinking a lot and I was spending all my money on drinking and so was my wife. We both went out drinking and that was all we were doing. We were so fed up with our jobs and we were pushing ourselves to the breaking point. We were deciding that the cop life wasn't for us. There was nothing that was making us happy and there was nothing that gave us any joy anymore. There was another cop that had killed himself because this case was too stressful on him. There was just too much pressure to solve this case and he couldn't take it anymore. He left his wife and two kids behind and he was a good father to them. He was father of the year to his kids according to his wife and I was going to go to his funeral because we were old friends. I went to the funeral and there were about a hundred people and it was a good turnout I would say. I was investigating a crime when I got called to another crime and it was weird. I had just got done investigating this crime and this crime was a couple hours old. It was a doctor and it was a girl that was twenty three. She was Samantha Todd and she was a pretty girl. She was just a young girl and I was amazed. She was very smart from what the other doctors said. She was one of the best doctors they had and she was good at her job. They thought she was going to make it a long time at her job but that wasn't the case. That was just the killer's way of saying she had to die early. Everyone has their day to die and she had her day to die and that was today. The next kill was an oral hygienist and he was the best oral hygienist in town. He had all his tools and he was the best people person you could find in three counties. There was nothing that he didn't talk about and he was great at getting to know people. There was a good dentist gone and another would replace him and he wasn't going to be as good but he would do. There was nothing that made sense about this because it was like she wanted to kill the best people at their jobs and she was being a dick about it. Did she even visit the dentist? Maybe she didn't if she killed the best dentist in the town. She was just cruel for doing it. There was a dentist and eventually he turned out to better at his job than the other dentist and it was surprising to me. The next kill was a first responder and she was always the first to show up at our crime scenes. We would have to find another one and it was like she was killing people that we had to replace. I didn't know how she was doing it. She was doing it quite often and it was happening more often than the dentist and the first responder. It was our cops and firefighters and it was our best doctors and it was our best emergency surgeons and it was getting out of control. The next kill was going to be the important kill that was going to get to me and I was going to blow a gasket. I was just going to lose my mind. I was going to lose my cool in front of everybody and they were going to tell me to calm down. I was going to have to walk away from the crime scene. They were going to ask me if I was alright and I wasn't going to answer because all the cases were getting to me. I was colliding with a wall and getting a concussion because it was all downhill from here. I wasn't going to stop until all these cases were closed. If one of these cases were solved that means all of these cases were related. There was nothing that made sense about these cases. We didn't know how she was choosing her victims because it could be random or it could be a special hatred for every one of these victims. I didn't know of any theories that we had but we continued to look at the last case and thought about the sweat on the volume knob. We had no leads and we weren't getting anywhere with the tip lines. It was like we couldn't catch a break but we were still hopeful and it wasn't like we were completely in the dark. There was always a lead out there, we just needed a young hopeful detective to find it. There was something that bothered me, the serial killer was going to reveal herself and it hadn't happened yet. I was waiting patiently and I was getting annoyed and I was sick of waiting so I decided to do some sleuthing of my own and found a stolen car the killer had used. There was a note in there addressed to me with her handwriting. There was also a handwritten letter sent to my house with some weird messages on it and I didn't like that she knew my wife's name. I memorized all the letters that the serial killer had wrote me and it was like it was haunting me and keeping me up at night. I don't think it was going to get any better. I was going to get something out of this whether it was satisfaction or a sense of pride or justice or something along those lines. It had to something that was worth it and it was going to be something that was going to make me happy. I was six feet from the edge ready to jump from a very high building and it was depressing and it was a good thing I didn't jump. There was nothing to save me from that ledge but myself and that ledge was always going to call me from now on. That ledge was like the serial killer, taunting me and wanting me to be sucked in by all the depression and hatred brought on by what I see in myself. I was getting this itching feeling that it was a family member. I was in a trance when I looked up at the body and came down to earth. Someone had to snap me back into reality and only then did I realize it was something that I couldn't get back. It had to be my sister because that was the only logical answer. Or it could be my dad he was old enough to commit the crimes and he was seventy and I was fifty two. I was going to make this count when I caught him. There was nothing that made me want to make this next case have clues and make this serial killer screw up so we could catch her. She wasn't going to screw up until she wanted to and even then her fingerprints weren't in the system and that was a fact. She had never been convicted unless it was a petty crime and it was going to be hard to convict her of all the crimes instead of just one crime. I was just frustrated I couldn't catch one serial killer and it was going to be a long time until we were going to catch her. We were going to catch her in a few years and that was a promise for all the victims. It was going to be a good conviction. There was going to be a good case where there was bad people dying. It didn't matter how hard we tried, we had no evidence and we weren't catching this serial killer and I was bottling up all my emotions in this case. In the end this case the forensics won out. We had none and it was going to solve the case. There were a lot of cases. It was around seventeen thousand and some and it was so many that it was taking so much space. It was taking up rooms and it was just getting to the point where I was fifty seven and my wife was fifty two. It was just going to make us have stress over our heads. We were trying to deal with all the stress of our jobs and it was keeping us sane but we were going insane. It was a double edged sword. It was a contradiction that we needed to work on. We needed a vacation and our bosses wouldn't let us take a vacation until we retired. It was like we were slaves to our jobs. We were slaves to our jobs because our bosses were slave drivers. We were being worked day and night and we weren't getting any breaks. It was getting us into a rut. There was nothing that we liked and there was nothing that we were getting out of our jobs. There was nothing good about my job and I was about to retire. I was going to make this my number one priority to find out who was related to me and who wanted to kill all these people. There was nothing that I wanted more than to kill this serial killer. No one would let me do that. No one would let me do that and that would piss me off. I was going to kill her anyways whether it was self-defense or not. It was nothing that I was going to be proud of but it had to done. I had to investigate these kills committed by this serial killer because I was lead investigator. I was honored but it was also a lot of pressure. The kill I was investigating was a lacrosse player and it was a high school player. He was a good player and he scored six goals yesterday. I would say that was pretty good for such a small net. I was impressed and I was going to have my kids in high school soon. It was nice because they were growing up so fast and we could have some time to ourselves for a little bit. They were gone until four and we could have sex for a couple of hours. It was nice and it was like we were jackrabbits. We were always having sex while the kids were at school. They were learning a lot and they were getting B averages. They were smart and they were doing decent. They were liking their teachers for the most part. There were some teachers that they didn't like but other teachers were great. They had fun with most of their teachers at school and that was what made school fun. We had their friends at the house and we were very friendly. We didn't embarrass them when their friends were over like most parents did. We were cool parents when their friends were over and we served good food. Their friends liked like tacos in a bag, and it was a good meal time. We had them over a lot and we served these meals over time. They were in love with us and they ate like royalty when they were over. We only ate like that when they were over. Other than that we ate normal food. It was good food and it was food that we ate. We ate breaded shrimp that was good and it was like we were heaven. We were eating really good that night and we had halibut and that was the best fish to have. It was my favorite fish and we went fishing all the time. We all had fun and it was something for the family and friends to do for social activity. We were eating very good food. We needed a good meal like this because we were eating plain meals and we needed something different. We were just getting burnt out on eating the same meals all the time. There was nothing I liked more than halibut and it was cooked just right and it was the best.

The next kill was a pimp and he was dressed in a purple suit and orange pants and he was dressed in flashy clothes. He was just looking weird and it was like he was trying to impress someone. It wasn't working for me. It was like a showoff statement and it wasn't like he was showing off for anyone around here. There was nothing about this that was making sense. Why did she kill a pimp? She hadn't killed very many pimps before. In fact I think it was her second pimp she had killed. It was weird but I guess she didn't have to have a reason for killing the people she killed. I was going to investigate this with no clues or forensic evidence. I was baffled that this was only her second pimp killed. It was like she didn't care to kill pimps. She didn't mind pimps apparently. Maybe pimps didn't bother her and cops and firefighters did. Who knows? She killed another cop and that brought the cop count total to thirty in all. That was a lot for a serial killer. He was shot with his own gun under his pillow and it was kind of ironic. I found it ironic but none of the other cops thought so when I brought it up. I was wondering why she had killed so many cops but she had killed more firefighters. There was firefighters that had been set on fire. In fact they had all been set on fire and there was forty that had been set on fire. It was a higher number than the cops by far.

There was a football player that didn't have a head. He was probably eighteen and he was getting a scholarship to Notre Dame to be a Tight End. There was other small schools that wanted him but he wanted Notre Dame because they were a good school. That was his first school and they were his only choice out of the smaller schools that wanted him. He was very smart and he wanted something more. He didn't know what that was. He was going to be something some day and then he got killed. He was a good talented football player before he died. I wish he could have went to Notre Dame to play football. Now he would never get that chance. His family was mad as they should be. They were asking what we were doing and we told them the truth. There wasn't much we could do without evidence. They were mad with the answer. It was better than sugarcoating it and it was better than telling them we were doing everything we could like we told everyone else. It was all bullshit in the end and it was all good intentions. It going to shit and it was going to make us look like shit cops. There was something that was troubling me how could the serial killer go this long without leaving a clue? There was nothing that made sense about that. We were at the end of the rope and it was like we were looking in the mirror wondering what we were seeing. We were seeing failure and disappoint. We were getting a sword to the stomach and we were getting a bullet to the head. It was instant death. There was no inspiration to keep us going. There was nothing to do but choose your job or see your kids grow up. I say that because I was working so many hours now that I wasn't getting home until dark. I was working fifteen hours and it was taking its toll. There was nothing that was good about that because I had to drink a lot of energy drinks and coffee to stay awake and sleep six hours. That wasn't enough because I was running on fumes. There was nothing I could do because I was just going to have to deal with it if I wanted my job. I was just getting my feet wet. I was working all these hours and still not catching this serial killer. It was around the clock and it was like they wanted to kill me with all these hours. It was like they were trying to drain my battery. They wanted me to get this serial killer on nothing. There was nothing that made sense about any of these cases. There were all these cases and none of them were going to get solved. I needed evidence that I didn't have and I was the only one in the office investigating the crimes. It was depressing and they were going to move me back with the people that were investigating the crime. I felt alone on this case and I wanted out. I wanted to work at Wal-Mart because it was better than this. I wanted to get paid eighteen dollars an hour for distribution. It was more than I was getting paid as an investigator. It was sad and I needed more money as an investigator. I saw a hobo dead in an alley and he was asphyxiated. He was dead within seconds and he was in his twenties. His name was Randy Parker and he was just a kid. He was scrounging around for money. His parents were giving him money from time to time but they wouldn't support him to help him live in an apartment. They wouldn't help him find a job but the money part was nice. He would blow it on booze and then when they figured this out they stopped giving him money. He started stealing and went to jail. He got the easy life and got free food. He liked that and with the free food he wasn't a hobo anymore. He was living the good life in his mind. He was getting good food in his mind and he was getting royal treatment. In his mind he was safe and loving it. There was no dangers in jail for him and he was just cozy in there. He was just loving it there. He got out of jail and got himself killed. It was a tragedy for him but he was starving and it was a better place for him. It was better than starving and living the life of a hobo. It was better than suffering on the streets. He was just miserable and he didn't know what to do for food because not too many people were throwing away food.

The next person to die was a hooker and she was a brunette. She was a hooker that was very active and she was very unclean. She was infected with many diseases and she passed it on to many husbands. They would pass it onto their spouses and they would cheat on husbands. It would be a vicious cycle and it was terrible. It was like a cycle that never broke. If they would get tested they could get pills if there were pills or they would have to live with it. There were just so many disease ridden hookers. It was a terrible world out there and it was a good thing I had a wife. There was a good thing that was going for me.

I went to a strip club and had sex with one of the strippers. It was great because she knew what she was doing. She was very pretty and I put good cologne on. The wife was turned on by the cologne. We had sex and we were role playing. It was very sexy. We were the best at role playing. We were pros and we were good at our sex voices. We were going at it for three minutes and we were exhausted. We went at it for another ten minutes and then we were done. It was all over and we were going to work the next day for another ten hours. We were becoming more satisfaction from our jobs. There was something we were missing from our jobs and that was the passion. We needed that passion and we knew that passion had been missing for a while. There was something we needed to do to get it back but we didn't know what we could do to get it back. There was nothing we could do to get it back in our minds that we could think of. We were getting stressed from our jobs and it wasn't fun anymore. It was getting bad enough where we were having fights over the smallest things. There were things that we shouldn't be fighting about but it was the small things that were making us mad. It was the fact that we wanted to get out of our jobs now. We wanted to stop fighting over the little things. It was things like whose turn is it to do laundry, and it's your turn to load the dish washer and things like that. We were just fighting to fight. It was our jobs and nothing else mattered besides the fights. It wasn't anything more than the stress of our jobs. There was nothing that made me feel worse than yelling at my wife. I was doing it constantly and she was yelling at me like it was a grudge match. I wanted to see my friends and she was controlling me not letting me see them. If she did she wanted to go with me. It was like if I see them you aren't coming with me. She said how do I know you aren't going to cheat on me? I was just getting frustrated and I was burying my head in my hands and rolling my eyes. I was slamming the door shut and walking out and drinking at the bar. I didn't care for her attitude and it was like I couldn't talk to her anymore. It was like I couldn't have a real conversation with her without having a fight. We were fighting every day after we came home from work. It was like we were little kids having a temper tantrum. It was just like we went back in time machine and we were five years old again. We stopped fighting for a couple of days and then we started again. Then I started drinking at the bars more frequently and my wife started joining me. We stopped fighting for a while and it was great. There was nothing I liked more than a marriage without fights. It was like a room with peace and quiet. I was watching forensic files with Sarah and it was relaxing. It was just what we needed to calm down. We were relaxed and it was like we were Zen. We needed this to relax when we came home. We were always relaxing when we came home. We had no stress when we came home and it was nice. We weren't having sex as often as we used to but I didn't care. I had confidence and getting the cases closer to solved. There was shoeprints in the blood. It was all coming together and there were shoes left at the crime scene that were fairly new. They were the killers. They were fairly new on the market and we tracked them down. Not many people buy them. There were a hundred and we narrowed it down to girls. There were twenty and one was two family members. One was my sister and one was my wife and I couldn't determine which one it was. It was going to be a hard decision. I was pretty sure I knew which one it was but the surprise was too good to be true. It couldn't be my sister because my sister was in a different town. I knew I couldn't arrest my own wife until I knew for sure. I checked for sure and then I knew this was it. She had stolen all the cars and the money was never found. The writing didn't match her writing and that made no sense. Then I remembered that she had changed her writing. She could change her writing by writing with her other hand and that made sense. She changed her writing to mine and it was nice. It looked like mine and it was just like mine. It was a perfect match to mine and I kept the letters. It was matching my handwriting and I had to arrest her soon. I followed her and I saw her kill a few people. I knew it was her and I took pictures and it was close enough to zoom in the camera. I got a picture of her face. I was going to send the photos to the papers and it was going to incriminate her in every crime. It was going to make her the bad guy. It was going to prove she was the serial killer. There was nothing that was going to get her out of this. It was going to make her look like a fool. It was going to make her look like an amateur. I took the photographs proving that she had committed these murders. It was going to make her know that I was the cop that caught her. There was no doubt that it was going to be hard to arrest my own wife. It was going to make me sick. It was going to make it hard to tell her that I knew she was the serial killer. She was going to know I knew at some point from my behavior. I was acting weird at home and she was noticing. She was asking what was wrong and when I said nothing she knew I was lying. She gave me a back massage and kissed me on the lips and she gave me a massage. She asked me what was wrong and again I said nothing and she got mad. She said if we couldn't communicate then we had secrets and secrets were just as bad as lying. I said I knew who the serial killer was and I said it was a family member. I said it was going to be hard to arrest them. She said that I had to do what I had to do no matter how hard it was. There was nothing that was going to be easy about this but it was going to be done soon. I took pictures of all my wife's kills and I took copies of all of them. It was hard but I knew I had to. I was keeping them in the safe in which I only knew the combination. There was nothing that she knew about the safe. She didn't even know about the safe or where it was. That was the best thing because then she would know the combination and she would know about the pictures. There were two copies of the pictures and I kept them in the safe. It was in two safes and it was the best thing I had ever thought up. It was a master plan and I was a genius for thinking of taking pictures of her at the crime scene. She was the culprit in all of this and I needed to know that she was the criminal. I was afraid to sleep with the enemy because if she knew I was taking pictures of her. I could be next. I was going to be next in her sick killing plot. There was going to be no doubt about that and she was going to kill anyone that got in her way.

The next kill she made was a high school basketball player. He was eighteen years old and he was making twenty points a game. That was pretty good and he was going to go to a good college on a scholarship. He got killed before that could happen and his parents held out hope until he got killed. They were infuriated because his dreams were crushed and their star was so bright. Now it was dim and burnt out. It was so dim that it was fizzled out. It was like it the star had just gone out. I was sad that a basketball star had died because he had so much promise. He could have gone to almost any college he wanted. It was his future ahead of him and he was dead before he could enjoy his life. He was a good kid and he didn't deserve to die and either did these other victims. I was fed up with all this killing and I wanted it to stop. It was going to be soon because I was going to drop the hammer on my wife's head soon. I was gathering all the pictures to convict her. She didn't know it and that was the best part. She was the best serial killer I had ever met but in the last couple of days she had become sloppy. She should have known I was watching her and she knew better than that. When I was watching her and taking pictures of her I felt like I should have been stopping her. I knew taking pictures was better. This was better and this was going to be what convicted her. This was going to make the case and it was going to make me the hero. It was going to make me the best cop in the division and it was going to make me captain. I was going to turn it down to retire and vacation. I was going to retire in the Cayman Islands and it was going to be sweet. I don't know if I could afford it unless I bought a cheap house. I could do something like drink and have a good time. My retirement would pay for it and it was going to be a blast. I was going to make it a party and I was going to party like a rock star. It was going to be fun. I was all about fun and drinking was fun for me. It wasn't going to be fun drinking with a serial killer especially when I was sleeping with one. I started sleeping on the couch because I was staying up late. I didn't want to sleep with a serial killer and it was creepy. It was creepy sleeping with a serial killer and the whole thing seemed weird to me. She killed a doctor next and it was a heart surgeon. He was the best in town and I caught it on camera. I made copies and I was prepared to send it to the media. The police were going to love it and praise me. She was killing him in his house and I was outside. I took pictures of her coming out of the house. It was incriminating with it being dark but it was clear that it was a stolen car. It was a nice car that had her fingerprints on the steering wheel. I loved that she was making these mistakes. There were usually no mistakes made by my wife but she was making a lot of mistakes. It was unlike her and she ditched her stolen car and I took fingerprint tape and put it in my safe. It was a perfect fingerprint lift and it was great. It was great and it was going to be the best evidence we could get. There was going to be a mountain of evidence against her and it was going to make her get into a lot of trouble. I was going to send the fingerprint tape to the forensics lab they would match it to Sarah.

The next person Sarah killed was a Firefighter and she set him on fire like usual. It was with gasoline and it was a very excruciating death. I imagined he suffered in the worst possible way. He was suffering every second that he was on fire. He tried to stop, drop and roll but he couldn't put himself out because grass couldn't put out a fire. That was a tragedy that he had to die that way. By the time someone threw water on him he was crisp. It was too late because he was burnt up and dead. There was nothing anyone could do for him. His family cremated what was left of him. There was nothing worse than being lit on fire and drowning. It was worse to burn alive and suffer. I couldn't imagine the pain but I caught it all on camera because it was all in the fire house. I ran out of the fire station and got in the car and drove off. I got the evidence home and she didn't know it was me. I was a ghost at that point and I was good at not being noticed. I was good at being a ghost like that. I went home and acted normal and she didn't suspect a thing. We were watching forensic files and she wondered what was in the safe. She wondered what the combination was and I knew when she was watching. I made sure she was sleeping when I put the evidence in the safe. I was careful and made sure she was sleeping. and I knew she would never figure out the combination. I was going to sleep when she asked what was in the safe. I said nothing that was important just work stuff. I needed it for work and I couldn't share it with her because I was the only one that could see it. These eyes have bled for this evidence for a long time. The guys would just ask questions. I was just trying to avoid a fight but she kept asking questions and I wasn't going to answer. I went to bed. She was very pushy and I didn't want to answer. She was just being a bitch. I was going to be a wall and not give an inch. Before the next kill I was going to catch her in the act. I was going to get her and I was going to be the hero. It was going to be the end of my act and the end of my story. I was going to make a little bit of money. She was about to kill a surgeon in the hospital and I pulled out a gun. I was about to say something and she turned the gun on me.

"So you know I'm the killer."

"I knew it from the moment I looked at the photos of the teenager that burnt down the church."

"Your smart but you have no evidence so your

screwed and I was a teenager so the time on that case has run out."

"That's where it all started and this is where it is going to end."

We both shot at the same time and we were dead. Every cop rushed in and there was blood everywhere. The serial killer was caught after nineteen thousand kills and it was a reign of terror that ended with me dead, a serial killer dead our kids without parents. They ended up with my sister. They grew up and one went into forensics and the other became a teacher.

Printed in the United States
By Bookmasters